AM I IN THE RIGHT PLACE?

AM I IN THE RIGHT PLACE?
BY BEN PESTER

BOILER HOUSE PRESS

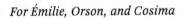

For Émilie, Orson, and Cosima

ORIENTATION

'There you are! And you've had a baked potato, good.'

You turn away from your screen and look up. A man is there – a tall man, thin and spectacled. From where you are sitting, you can see almost into the black slipper-soles of his nostrils.

'Graham?'

'That's right, I'm Graham. Ready for your orientation?'

'Yes, I think so!'

'Good,' says Graham. 'Good-good-good.'

You realise that you've seen him already today – this Graham. He was in the unisex toilets at about ten a.m. He was using moisturiser on his hands, humming quietly as he massaged the cream into the skin between his long fingers. You remember his relentless technique, the way he see-med to find it musical, the amount of cream he was using, and his humming, which struck you as both joyless and secretive.

'You've read the documentation I sent to you?' Graham asks.

The documentation he is referring to is a PDF called *Finding Your Feet*. So far, you have managed to scroll to the end, just to see how long the document is (657 pages including appendices). You have read the first forty or so pages. This covered the sections entitled:

- *Overview*
- *Introduction*
- *Welcome*
- *Getting Started (A Check List)*
- *Here You Are*
- *Hi There! – A View From the Leadership Team*

As you examined the *First Things First* section, you were gripped by a sensation that you were melting. Actually melting. It was during the melting phase that you decided to take a break and buy a baked potato from the little van outside. Most of it is still in the Styrofoam box on your desk, cold and too hard to eat.

'Well, I've read a good chunk of it,' you say.

'Oh good – which sections, exactly, have you read?'

When you tell him the sections you have read, Graham looks disappointed.

'But I really think I got a good sense of what's expected of me,' you say. 'I'm keen to get my orientation done, you know? I have been told that it's an essential part of the onboarding process and –'

'Have to interrupt you there,' Graham says. 'The onboarding process begins *after* your orientation.'

'Right, yes. I just mean, I came from an agency, and they were quite vague about the role, so I am keen to meet my line manager and that sort of thing.'

Graham raises his eyebrows. He checks his clipboard.

'You're writing the training material. That's what I have here.'

'Well, yes, but that's very broad,' you say. You start explaining that you need to know some key details before you can really do that work. Graham listens for a moment or two, but then becomes visibly bored.

'I think we should get on,' he says, cutting you off just as you were explaining about the essential need to identify the key stakeholders for the training material.

'Oh sure, you say.' Sure-sure-sure. 'Sorry. I'm just –'

'Just what?'

You let out a breath and decide to just be honest about how you are feeling. 'Sorry,' you say. 'I had a long journey here this morning. I feel a bit lost, to tell you the truth.' You tell Graham about your difficulty finding this office, and how you seemed to have been in a GPS black hole as you walked between here and the station – getting lost in the same industrial mews three times before you eventually called a taxi you could not afford. Graham looks bored again, so you repeat quickly that you are just keen to find your feet.

'Maybe,' he says, smiling, 'if you had read all of *Finding Your Feet*, you would know where they are!'

'Ha,' you say.

'Yes, funny things, haha,' Graham says. 'Just to give you an overview of the format, this orientation is tailored especially to your needs. I have studied your profile and the requirements of your role to get an idea of what you require.'

You tell Graham you think that sounds great. You tell him that normally these things are just, 'There's the fire escape. There's the first aid blanket. Here's a list of marshals.'

'Marshals are important,' Graham says. He puts a finger to his lips in contemplation. 'We don't have a first aid blanket. The heat blanket and the dehydration blankets are in the first aid kits. But that is not part of your orientation.'

He is looking at you now, somewhat expectantly. You don't know what to do. It feels like he might say 'Let's begin,' or something, but he doesn't.

During this awkward moment, you notice that his apple green tie is incredibly long. It rides smoothly over his thin but undulating body, over his pale grey belt. The wide chevron of it points to his balls.

'Ready then?' Graham says.

You nod. 'Yeah, sure.'

'Good. This way.'

Graham walks away and you have to rush to catch up with him.

As you follow Graham around the office, something about his speed gives you a weirdly urgent need to talk. You spout on about how glad you are to be here finally. You tell him it feels like you have been answering security questionnaires and pre-screening questions for literally months since being offered the job. Even though actually it has only been six weeks, and most of that was waiting for one of your referees to come back from holiday.

'I read all your references. Very impressive. No trouble there.'

'Thank you,' you say, even though it's a surprise that Graham would have any business looking at your references. He's just the health and safety guy, isn't he?

'That's good to hear,' you say.

'Very impressive what some people said about you,' Graham repeats. 'Very creative, they said.'

You wonder which of your previous employers would have described you as creative, and what they would have meant by it. Your job is not about creating anything; it's about producing accurate, relevant material for a specific audience.

Graham stops abruptly next to a desk. It's a normal enough desk, at which there sits a slim, pale man. He is wearing a sad-looking white shirt and black trousers. He has eye sockets that look much too big for his eyes. Graham seems like he is about to speak to the man – he even rests a hand on the man's shoulder. But in fact, he is just using the man as something to lean on while he talks to you.

'Have you eaten?' Graham asks.

'Yes, I had a jacket potato.'

'Oh yes. Of course! I saw the box. Cheese'n'bean, was it?'

'Yes. Cheese'n'bean, I think that's right.'

'Excellenté!' Graham says. He mwah-kisses his fingers, spins on his heel and sets off again with renewed speed. You leave the pale man with an apologetic smile, and catch Graham as he prowls past various pods of desks. He is talking to you over his shoulder, saying,

- 'Bins
- Recycling
- Window
- Box storage
- Bulk items
- Sales team bin.'

You appear to be heading towards the kitchen area.

'Are we going upstairs?' you ask. 'I heard that the team I'm working with are on the second floor?'

'Just this way first, to the kitchen and food preparation area.'

You tell him that someone already showed you the kitchen area when you first arrived.

'Not properly,' Graham says making a note on one of his clipboards.

'*This* is the kitchen area,' he announces. 'Ah, you can see. Coffee. Tea there. Cups in this cu– oh. Well, normally there are cups in this cupboard. If you can't find any here, you may have to look in the dishwasher, which is here. Or in the sink. Sometimes people leave cups in the sink.'

You nod. You say, 'Sure. Got it.'

He starts touching the taps on the sink with the flat of his hand. 'This is the water for washing up. This one here is for making coffee. It's attached to a boiler, see? It's always hot, so be careful because you might burn yourself if you try to use this for washing up.'

'I'll remember that,' you say.

The tap Graham is referring to has a massive sign on it that says, *Do not use for washing up*, and has a hand-drawn figure covered in burning liquid. The figure is visibly screaming. The eyes are wide with horror and agonising pain.

'Please familiarise yourself with the safety message on the hot water tap, and the boiler more generally,' Graham says.

Aside from the hand-made sign, the boiler is a normal boiler. A white box with a large ugly dial on it. There is a dirty mark where someone has peeled away a sticker. A long thin pipe with a tap pokes out of the bottom. You have been looking at it now for well over twenty seconds. It's a fairly depressing object.

Graham is still watching you. 'Do you want to try it?' He says.

'You mean the tap? I guess I could. Sure.'

You reach out a hand to turn the tap on the boiler, but

Graham stops you.

'No,' he says sharply. 'Don't actually touch it. It's best if you simply enact the process. You can just improvise. No need to waste water.'

'You want me to just pretend?'

'Improvise, yes. Or enact.'

You approach the sink and pretend to wash up an imaginary cup using the water boiler, then pretending to realise the danger of using boiling water to wash up with, you stop and pretend to wash up using the correct tap.

You look at Graham. 'Like that?'

'I'd say you're about fifty percent of the way there.' Graham gestures towards the draining board.

You place the imaginary cup onto the washing up rack on the draining board and flick imaginary water off your hands. You do the water flicking as a kind of joke.

'I'd use a cloth to dry your hands, usually,' Graham says. 'Too much flicked water can cause slippages.'

He moves to another area of the kitchen.

'There's a microwave over there,' he says. 'So you can heat up food or whatever. Some people use it to warm their hot drinks. I personally find myself in so many meetings –' Graham's hands are now juggling the air '– that my tea goes cold and needs to be reheated three or four times before I actually manage to, ah, to drink it.'

Someone comes in – it's Craig. You met Craig when you came for your interview. In the interview, he introduced himself along with his job title, but you can't remember what it is, or what you said to him, or what he said to you. You do remember that throughout the interview he looked mostly at the backs of his own hands.

Craig is holding some Tupperware. He says hello to

you, and hello to Graham. He says, 'Excuse me,' and you shuffle out of his way so he can get to the microwave.

'Yes, stand back,' Graham says, looking down at where your feet are and inching backwards himself, as though there is some kind of safety line on the floor. Then to Craig he says, 'We're just observing, please continue.'

Craig thanks him again then puts his Tupperware into the microwave.

Graham whispers, 'Watch how Craig uses the microwave. See how he places the Tupperware container into the oven with the lid slightly loose. That is very important. Then he closes the door. Then he uses the dial to select the amount of time to cook it for. Try to memorise this, if you can. Although the full manufacturer instructions for this microwave model are included in the *Finding Your Feet* documentation, which you still have to read.'

To Craig, in a much louder voice, Graham says, 'What have you got today then, Craig?'

Craig reacts to Graham's question by stopping the microwave and removing the Tupperware. He opens it and wordlessly reveals, first to Graham, then to you, what's inside. Craig's Tupperware pot is squirming with noodles, shredded spring onion and floppy strips of red and yellow peppers, all collected together in a sort of shiny glue.

Craig details the recipe, describing the method he used to create the dish. He talks about it for almost five minutes, providing a lot of detail and making a lot of gestures. He uses the word 'bosh' and many other loud and destructive-sounding verbs to describe how you cook the noodle dish he is now, once again, reheating in the microwave. He also uses the word 'banging' to describe how it tastes.

'That sounds delicious, doesn't it?' Graham says to you.

'How long will you microwave that for then, Craig?'

'Eleven minutes.'

'Wow,' you say. 'Eleven minutes! Is it frozen?'

'No,' Craig says.

'Remember, of course, that we don't put anything metal into the microwave,' Graham says.

Graham and Craig move closer together and jointly watch the Tupperware full of noodles go round and round in the microwave. There is quite a smell now, in the kitchen, coming from the microwave. It doesn't seem to register with either Graham or Craig, but it reminds you of being at a childhood friend's house for dinner one time and wishing you could go home.

As Craig's food rotates, you find yourself remembering how that wash of homesickness swept over you, and the small tremulous panic of knowing you couldn't leave. It's strange how far into the memory you go. You remember that your friend... James? His name was James. James would not let you ask his father to take you home. He said it would be too much trouble. Even though you should be focusing on the safety advice in the kitchen area, you struggle to stop thinking about that boy, and his father boiling and boiling and boiling up that food. Sad little James.

You only snap out of it when you notice that Graham and Craig are standing so close to each other that their cheeks are almost touching as they watch the food turning in the microwave. The timer on the microwave says there are still 03:09 minutes left until the end.

Shaken by the memory of sad James and his father, you turn your gaze away from Craig and Graham, and explore the off-white walls. They are mostly bare except for a few angry red and grey food stains above the little eating table. There is a notice board covering the wall beside the cupboards and the sink.

You step closer to the board and start reading. There is a sponsorship poster for someone called Dean, who is raising money for cancer research. Dean is planning to walk a marathon at night, it says, through the city. You cannot see which city; it doesn't seem to say. Next to Dean's sponsorship poster is a sponsorship poster for someone else – this time it's Martin. Martin is raising money for testicular cancer. He will also do a marathon, but in the daytime, and will run the marathon in the traditional way. You reckon you can probably spare some money, you think. But you will clear it with your partner first, since there have been some worrying conversations in the dark between you recently, just before you fall asleep.

Underneath these two posters is an advert for a car valeting service called Car-Man-Geddit.

'It's a nice kitchen,' you say, hoping to be able to move on, but also not wanting to ruin the moment for Craig and Graham, who are still standing incredibly close to each other, rapt by the turning of the noodles.

'I like the notice board. I might sponsor Dean, maybe.'

Graham is still watching the microwave. You hear him whisper something into Craig's ear. Something like, 'There you are.'

'I know,' Craig says.

The microwave finally bleeps and Graham snaps back into life. 'Shall we get on?' he says, moving away from Craig.

You nod. Then, as an afterthought, you say, 'Before I forget, Graham, could you give me some walking directions for the best way back to the station? I got quite lost on my way here and had to pay for a taxi.'

Graham raises his eyebrows and shakes his head, as if he cannot believe what you have said. 'You were sent a very good map,' he says.

You are about to tell him that you were not sent any such map, but he starts talking again. 'As I'm sure you have guessed, there is the ground floor kitchen fire escape to look at next.'

After a look at the fire escape, which is a door in the corner of the kitchen, Graham leads you back through the office to the stairwell. The door to the stairwell requires a security pass. Graham stands up on tiptoe and thrusts out his pelvis to get the pass that is attached to his belt onto the pass reader.

'Most people choose the necklace lanyard type for their blue badge,' he says, 'but I prefer the more secure belt hoop lock. Of course, my badge has access to more areas than yours, so it's probably safe for you to have the necklace type.'

You tell him whatever is easiest is fine with you.

On a small landing between flights of stairs, Graham gestures to the window. 'Come and look out of this window. Many bird varieties have reportedly been seen from this vantage point.'

'Oh really?'

'Yes, really. I haven't seen all of them myself, but all of the sightings have been from reliable sources. Daphne, who you won't know, saw a young egret with its mother just last month.'

You approach the window and look out.

'If you look closely at the willow tree,' Graham says, 'just there in the mid-range – about fifteen yards from the yellow pole. Can you see?'

You nod, even though you cannot see any such willow, or any such pole. The whole landscape is blank. Just grass, and fencing. In the distance you can see a few clumps of trees, but it's really not possible to discern willows. It's just trees.

'Well, just to the right of that willow is the rally-point in the event of a fire. You see, near the disused children's slide?'

You can see no such slide. You feel you really ought to tell Graham that actually there is a problem, maybe with the angle you are viewing from, or the perspective, because you cannot see the same things that he can see. Before you get the chance to speak, he holds up his hand.

'If you hear the fire alarm, which is a constant, high pitch siren, like this:

- eeeeeeeeeeeeeeeooooooowwwww
- eeeeeeeeeeeeeeeooooooowwwww
- eeeeeeeeeeeeeeeooooooowwwww
- eeeeeeeeeeeeeeeooooooowwwww
- eeeeeeeeeeeeeeeooooooowwwww
- eeeeeeeeeeeeeeeooooooowwwww

Then you are to leave through one of the fire escapes and head for that point.'

You still cannot see where he means, but then, you reason, if there ever is a fire you will just follow everyone else out of the building and go where they go.

'Are you now familiar with the fire muster point?' Graham asks.

'Er, yes?'

'Good.' Graham makes a mark on one of clipboards. 'What the hell?' Graham shouts suddenly. 'No! No! No-no-no-no-no!'

You flinch at the volume of his voice. You ask Graham what's wrong, but he acts as though you are not there. He continues to stare out of the window, his whole body is tense, ducking his head this way and that, as though watching something move. Every now and then he curses politely but firmly under his breath. You have no choice but to remain where you are while this goes on – you cannot see whatever outrage Graham can see. You cannot see a living soul, nor any detail whatsoever.

Graham gets out his phone and loudly taps out a message. 'Unreal,' he says to himself. 'Un-fucking-real.'

You try again to follow his gaze, but the sun has come out from behind a cloud and you are dazzled, and suddenly very hot.

'This way,' Graham mutters. He barges past you, knocking you out of the way, then springs up the next flight of stairs, taking them two at a time.

You rub the top of your arm as you follow Graham. You are short of breath and prickly by the time you reach the first floor.

Graham looks at you. 'Is there a problem?' he says.

'It's nothing really,' you say. 'I mean, I'm sure it was an accident, but you really bashed me back then. My arm hurts quite a lot actually.'

Graham doesn't acknowledge your pain. He nods, checks his clipboards then checks his phone angrily.

You feel quite disoriented.

'Let's go into the first floor now,' Graham says.

The first floor is nearly identical to the ground floor. Maybe the air is slightly cooler, and maybe the smell is slightly less depressing. Also, the computers look newer, which is probably also the reason it smells different. Otherwise, it is the same as downstairs.

'All the rooms on this floor,' Graham says, 'are named after sports cars.'

Ferrari is the biggest of these rooms. There is also a Lotus room and another that maybe says Triumph, but you can't quite see it properly.

Through the frosted glass wall of Ferrari, a heated discussion is taking place between eight or nine men wearing different coloured pastel shirts. One of the men, who is wearing an apricot shirt, breaks away from the heated discussion and clutches his face in his hands. He looks like he is experiencing serious despair. He notices that you are looking, takes his hands away from his face and stares intensely at you through the glass wall.

You look away and exaggerate the action of exploring the office space with your eyes. You can see several desks that still have tinsel on them, though it has not been Christmas for a long time and it will not be again for an almost equally long time. You can also see more than one Simpsons character, or scene, pinned to the dividers of the various working areas, but if you had to count them, you would not be able to. If you had to walk towards the picture of a specific scene or character from The Simpsons, you would not be able to do it either. You simply know that they are there.

You realise that Graham is no longer by your side. He is four rows of desks away, almost in the centre of the room, giving a woman in a blue cardigan a tender look. He is touching her on the arm. Both Graham and the woman have their eyes closed. They part and the woman places a dried oak leaf into Graham's open hand.

You think Graham is telling the woman that he is Orientating you.

The woman in the blue cardigan looks at you and nods very solemnly. She has more leaves in her hands.

Graham places the leaf she gave him into his trouser pocket. He tilts his head and smiles. The woman looks relieved, or perhaps pacified is more accurate. She moves from foot to foot. There are leaves all around her on the floor.

Abruptly, Graham is on the move again. He passes you, walking briskly towards the first floor kitchen area. Over his shoulder he says, 'I bet you're wondering what that was all about!'

'Well, yeah,' you say. 'Did she just give you a leaf?'

'She has given me many things.'

This appears to be the only explanation Graham is prepared to give you. 'This way!' he says. His walking speed has increased by about fifty percent. You have to canter to keep up with him. You try to ask him again, as you speed along the office floor, what is the best way to the train station?

Graham stops walking so suddenly that you almost crash into him. 'Why do you want to know that?' he says. 'Why do you keep asking me that?'

'Well, for when I go home.'

'But there are hours before the end of the day. You're here now.'

'Yes, but for later.'

'I don't see why you need to know. There isn't time for this sort of thing.'

He races off again, into the first floor kitchen.

This kitchen is virtually identical to the one downstairs. Graham still seems angry with you. He touches the different objects, says their names just like he did on the ground floor. He does not mention the huge table-football table that takes up most of the kitchen space, the only major difference between here and the ground floor. He talks loudly to be heard over the sound that the four men in their twenties are making as they play a rowdy game of table football.

- 'Boiler
- Microwave
- Window
- Sink
- Taps
- Lucid printout of boiler flume technical drawings for reference
- Cups.'

When he comes to the end of his list, the football match also seems to come to an end. The four players wave and nod to Graham as they leave.

'There you are, lads,' he says.

'Yep,' one of them says back. The others all nod.

Now that it's quiet, Graham turns to you with a half-smile.

'You'll like this,' he says. He moves to the wall opposite the sink and opens a floor-length cupboard door. You try to remember if there was a corresponding door in the kitchen downstairs, but you can't recall any details of that kitchen anymore.

Graham gestures for you to look inside the cupboard.

'This is the stationery cupboard,' he says. 'Watch this. This'll cheer you up!'

He enters the stationery cupboard, but not in a normal way. He seems to be imitating a train as he moves forward. He folds his arms at the elbow, puffs out his cheeks, and thrusts his folded arms back and forth. He progresses deep into the cupboard, making little puffing steam-engine noises. Once inside, he blows loudly through his mouth and comes to a slow stop at the far end of the cupboard.

He calls out to you from within the darkness, 'What am I?'

You give no answer. You just stare at the back of Graham's head and body. It seems easier than you would have expected to allow this silence to linger. You glance out of the kitchen window. You feel sure that this window faces the same way as the one in the stairwell, but the view is not the same. You can see hundreds of trees clumped with startling green leaves that seem to separate in the wind, revealing fields and far away sheep. There are employees out there, walking about in the leaves, kicking them into the air.

'You can come in if you like,' Graham says. 'There's a chair just inside the door, you can unfold it and sit down while you work out my little puzzle.'

Graham hasn't moved. He is standing completely still. When you don't reply, he says, 'Sit. Down. Please, OK?'

'OK, fine.'

You press into the stationery cupboard. You can smell Graham's different odours – washing up liquid, unscented hand cream, pine flavoured bleach.

'It will be very disappointing if I have to tell you the answer,' he says. 'What am I?'

In your pocket, your phone is vibrating. You think for an instant how exciting the outside world could be. It could be anyone – it could be good news about another job. It could be news that your partner has secured work, which would mean you don't need to extend any more lines of credit. And, for some reason, you imagine that it could be sad little James, the boy who's house you wanted to leave when his dad was cooking. Sad little James could be calling to remind you that, when you asked him if he could ask his Dad to take you home, not only did he refuse, but he left you alone in the room. He shut the door of the windowless room you were in, and from the outside turned off the light. So you sat in the dark. Sad little James, you think, could be calling you to remind you that you sometimes remember this moment of being in his smelly pitch black room and wonder if in fact you are still there now, and everything that has happened in the intervening years has simply been your imagination.

You remember that you sometimes think you are still in the dark room and have rapidly assembled a complex imagined world that includes:

- Electric cars
- Your entire secondary school, college and university education
- iPhones
- Sexual experiences
- Your partner's life story
- The true capabilities of the internet
- This orientation in this office
- The demise of Pop-Tarts
- Everything – all of it.

You don't answer the phone. You are afraid, you realise, of Graham's reaction. You are afraid of what is happening. The phone stops ringing.

'Why did that woman give you a leaf, Graham?'

'What? That isn't relevant now!' Graham's voice in the dark cupboard is strange and manic. 'Look closely at my body!' He says. 'Come on! I bet you could get it if you would just look. What am I?'

You still don't make any guesses. You clear your throat. You know what you should say, but you can't say it for some reason.

'I am stationary!' Graham shouts at last. His voice rings with triumph. 'Stationery! This is the stationery cupboard and I am stationary. It's a joke! You can laugh, you know:

- haha
- haha
- haha.'

Graham exalts in his punchline, then almost immediately leaves the stationery cupboard, flowing out of it in his soft, sensible way.

You are about to follow him, but he slams the door.

You are shut in the cupboard, in the dark.

'Graham, let me out, please.'

You can hear Graham's voice, but he seems to be talking to someone else. The other person sounds very familiar to you.

'Graham!' you shout. But he does not respond.

You hear him saying, 'Let's go and see the second floor,' before leaving you there, in the dark.

You hear the familiar voice saying, 'Sure, that sounds good.'

You stand in the dark,
reaching out and touching nothing.

Your hands do not even find
the reassuring touch of pencils
or spiral-bound notepads.

You can hear Graham say he
has a surprise for you.

'Let's go up to the second floor, shall we?' Graham says.

'Yeah, sure, that sounds good,' you say. You feel as though you have forgotten something.

You follow Graham back out to the stairwell. On the way past some toilets, without looking round he extends one of his arms towards them and says,

- 'Facilities.'

At the top of the stairs, Graham checks his reflection in the reinforced glass of the door. He licks his teeth.

You follow Graham around the second floor. He raises his arms and points at things but does not say what their meaning is, nor what they are for. He stops next to a photocopier and brushes his hand down the arm of an employee in her mid-thirties. He runs his hand up and down her arm four or five times, then pats it. She waits for him to stop, then picks up her photocopying.

'There you are,' he says to her.

The employee smiles and then takes her photocopying away. As she goes, you notice that the top page of the photocopying is just an entirely black rectangle. You look at Graham's face. He has raised his eyebrows and is smiling at you.

'Graham,' you say. 'Did something happen? I feel as though I've missed some steps.'

'We are doing your orientation, that's all. It has been a bit of a fuss, to be honest. You have been distracted, but it's OK now. Let's just go back downstairs,' he says. 'I have a surprise for you.'

You follow him back to the stairwell. He points up at the ceiling in the stairwell. 'There is an upstairs,' he says. 'But we won't do that today.'

Graham holds out an open palm towards the stairs, and you walk ahead of him. You only get a few steps before you hear his voice in your ear.

'Don't er– sorry. Could you not clutch the railing like that as we go back down the stairs? Thank you. In the event of a fire, that would have a negative effect on others, wouldn't it? How would they get past you?'

You let go of the railing, becoming aware of how tightly you have been holding on.

'You recognise this area here,' Graham says. 'It's reception of course. And... this is your blue ID card.'

Graham lifts an ID card on a blue lanyard from the counter of the reception area. He clears his throat, and then he places the lanyard around your neck, like he is awarding you a medal. His face almost touches yours as he drapes it on you. He lets out a little breath onto your skin.

'There,' he says. 'There you are.'

'Thank you,' you say, tapping the blue pass on your chest.

You tilt the pass upwards to examine the picture on it, of your face. You look at your name and your staff number. Your face in the picture is too small for your shoulders. The picture makes you feel very sad.

'Come out here, please.'

You stop looking at your face on the card and follow Graham out into the car park. He gestures in the direction of the fire mustering-point he mentioned earlier. Just as before, you do not clearly see where it is. Your conviction is strengthened that, in the event of an actual fire, you will simply become part of the herd. You will be in amongst them as you shuffle through the smell of burning plastics as all the photocopiers and servers and vending machines burn. There will be black smoke and the faint excitement of knowing you will get paid no matter what happens. There will be the soft, accidental loveliness of someone's smart-casual shoulder as you are buffeted forward in the crush.

You are still imagining the fire when you realise that Graham is leading you towards the back of the car park. 'We have time for a short recce of the town and surrounding area, if you like? I know you got lost on your way here from the station.'

'Yes, horribly lost,' you say. 'But it's just part of finding my feet, I suppose.'

'Yes, finding your feet – the comprehensive guide which you have not yet read. So, tell me, have you found them?'

You look down as a joke, about to say, 'There they are,' but a sort of blankness comes over you, and you can't see your feet. Then a bird like a big heron calls loudly overhead, and you look up. There is no bird. There is just Graham, smiling at you next to his car.

You are not sure why, and you are not sure that you should be, but you are getting into Graham's car. He is smiling at you as he holds open the door. You do up your seatbelt and wait for Graham to get in. He doesn't get in straight away, and you can't quite see where he has gone. You can hear the sound of him bumping against the car somewhere behind you. It feels like it would be impolite to fully spin round and look at him. Finally, he gets in, he seems out of breath.

'Sorry about that. Right, ready? Let's go. A little surprise.'

He hums a tune as he drives out of the car park. As you pass the office building, you see a face looking down at you from a small window near the roof. The face looks sickeningly familiar. You strain to look closer, but you are distracted by a young professional man wearing headphones and strutting towards the office complex. When you look back to the window, the face is gone. Your phone vibrates in your pocket. You reach into your pocket to answer the call, but Graham makes an abrupt, nasal sound which stops you in your tracks.

You ask Graham if he is feeling alright.

He says, 'Please don't use your phone during the orientation, unless it's an emergency.'

You tell him you didn't realise you were still doing the orientation.

'It's not for my benefit,' he tells you. 'But don't you think it would be a good idea to pay attention – we don't want you to get lost again, do we?'

You tell him you agree with him, and then you start laughing at how lost you were on your way to work, and how you are even more lost now than ever. Even after you have been oriented.

'Over there,' Graham says, ignoring your joke about being oriented, 'is the bakery some people like. They sell a range of different sandwiches, and baps. They have pastries too, of course. If you ask them, I think they still do toasted sandwiches. Do you like toasted sandwiches?'

You nod.

Graham nods too, as if you have given him the correct answer.

He tells you fillings:

- ham and cheese;
- mayonnaise with prawns;
- just cheese;
- two types of cheese; and
- hoi sin duck with mayonnaise.

'If you ask them,' he says, 'they will tell you which fillings are best in a toasty. Prawns and mayonnaise is nice in a toasty, I find, but they are reluctant to make it unless you ask very specifically, unless you actually insist upon it. They told me once that hot mayonnaise and prawns is not a good idea! I said to them, how ridiculous. Hot mayonnaise is delicious. In France, they keep it out, they don't put it in the fridge, it sits out in the sun. Hot mayonnaise is fine!' he shouts. 'Do you like hot mayonnaise?' he asks.

You clear your throat and you nod. 'Yes,' you say. Yes to hot mayonnaise, even though nothing could horrify you more than coagulated mayonnaise and steamy little prawns.

'They also have a selection of soft drinks, and an espresso machine,' Graham continues. 'You can get a cup of Americano there for one pound thirty. Over there, on the left, is The Smiling Pig. That's a pub we sometimes go to after work. A few of the guys from the second floor and me have a quiz team. We do the weekly quiz at The Smiling Pig, and also another pub, which you won't have seen, because it's in Wolkingham. One of the guys from the team has a sister in Wolkingham, and she sometimes cooks us all supper before the quiz. She is a very kind woman. Very kind.'

Minutes go by as Graham continues to drive the car in near silence, in and out of populated areas, occasionally pointing at another bakery and raising his eyebrows and saying something like, 'Medium sized sausage rolls in there.'

The populated areas become fewer and further apart. After a period of driving that feels desperately long, Graham pulls, quite suddenly into a car park.

You did not read the sign properly, but the main building looks like a hospital of some kind. Or perhaps a home. You sit there in silence for a moment after Graham turns

off the ignition. Graham doesn't move, just sits there
staring straight forward.

'You don't mind, do you? I find it hard to drive past
without stopping in.'

You say, 'No, of course not.'

Graham looks relieved.

You follow him into the low, single-story building.
Is it a hospital? You confirm to yourself that it must be.
Although the sign by the door calls it a Centre. The John
David Richards Trust Centre.

'Pot plant has been here for seven years,' Graham says.
Then, as you stroll through the corridors, he points things
out to you:

> - 'Tiles designed by children from a local school.
> - Mosaic from a factory.
> - That window is broken, you cannot open it
>   anymore.
> - Lemon smell here for some reason, always.'

You arrive eventually at a ward. The ward is almost
completely empty, but in a corner, in a cardigan, there
is a man. He has loose, leathery skin, and holes in his
ears where there once must have hung heavy jewellery.
His eyelids have eyelids. His smile is the smile of a nice
donkey. Wrinkled, faded tattoos peep out of his burgundy
pyjama top. Graham goes over to him and rests a hand on
his shoulder.

Graham whispers to you, 'This is James. He used to
be in the delivery team. There you are, James. Poor little
James,' Graham says.

James extends his massive smile. He has four gold
teeth on his top front set. The rest are a series of crags,
ranged in a sad gradient of grey to orange.

'He left us to go travelling in 2007. Almost immediately after completing his orientation. He took up with a curator, didn't you Jim? An art curator, you know? I thought you would like to meet James because you were talking about him earlier.'

'Was I?' You do not remember saying anything out loud about James. Sad little James from your past.

'Oh yes, on and on, about how you sometimes imagine that you are locked in a dark room and everything you think you are experiencing is simply a memory.'

'But, no, it was the other way around,' you say. 'I sometimes imagine that all of this is a dream.'

Graham ignores you, cutting away as if you have said something annoyingly dull. He turns back to the old man. 'Are you alright, James?' he says.

James nods his head. James, you think, must have been administered lots of drugs recently. Graham tells you about James's journey around Europe. He went to all the cities. He worked, occasionally, as a gallery assistant. He fell in with some Italians and some French people too. He ate good food. He learnt new languages.

'As you can see,' Graham says. 'He rather over did it. But I can still see you, James, in there. The old you. There you are.'

Graham nods and James nods, and both men smile and sniff. Graham holds one of James's long hands and squeezes it. With that, he spins on his smooth heeled shoes and leaves the room, or ward, you're not sure which.

And then, as you follow him out through the network of corridors, past other doors and rooms and curtains, you realise something very strange.

'Nobody works here! There are no staff or anything!'

Graham looks down at you as he strides through the corridors. His lips are tight. There is rage there, bunched in his smooth walk.

'I really thought you would have had something to say about James, actually, rather than the absence of the Centre staff. I really thought you and he would have had a connection, which is why I brought you all the way out here, using my own petrol. Doesn't it mean anything to you? The effort I have put in to show you this other creative person that I know? No. All you care about is "where's the train station?" "Who's phoning me up?" "Where have all the nurses gone?" I think you could be more grateful. Much, much more grateful.'

In the silence that follows, with Graham staring at you, you grope for an appropriate apology, but, emerging into the fumes and the bluster of the car park, your words are swallowed by the wind.

'Over there, of course, is the station.'

Graham flaps a hand towards some trees.

'As any idiot knows.'

AM I IN THE RIGHT PLACE?

A walk in the cold sun feels like just what I need before meeting up with Dad. I will get energy from the sun's rays, like a plant, I tell myself. I will be invigorated by the cold air like sportspeople, and dog walkers are invigorated. I tell myself these things in the way that Dad might have said them to me, when I was younger, and he almost never used his normal voice, but joke voices and everything was a joke.

He has already texted to say he will be a tiny bit late, and I have texted back to say, *Don't worry! I am already in the café I like! And I have my book, so really don't worry!*

In the text, which is a lie, of course, I also tell him about the book I am reading, and ask if he has heard of it. He says he has, but I don't believe him. I tell myself not to do this – not to question the poor man and his every action, but he is late. Whenever he is late, I get flustered.

He is always late.

Of course, I am his son, and so I am always late. I shouldn't let it matter, but it does. I walk faster. I must arrive before he does so I can prove that I was there on time and he was the only one of us who was late.

The sun has now gone behind a cloud. The cold is not bracing, but brutal.

I redouble my effort to walk even faster. I feel a few pricks of warmth coming up from my chest, to my neck. I feel my cheeks going red.

I will be really glad to get into the café. I tell myself I should not drink too much coffee before I see Dad. I wonder if he will like the café. I wonder if it is his kind of place. I want him to be comfortable.

I arrive at the café. It's so hot inside, my skin starts to itch. I feel out of breath and ridiculous, but my favourite table is available, so I dump my coat on the chair and go to the counter to order a large strong coffee.

They have a great deal of mid-century furniture in this café, and you can purchase nice mugs and tea towels and coffee makers and even light fittings, wrapping paper, bowls, mirrors, cards, and trinkets. I feel as though it will blow Dad's mind. He never goes to places like this. He barely leaves his own kitchen. He sits with his whiskey and his fruit flies.

I think about getting Dad a card. But then – why would I do that? Why would I want to present him with a card while he is forced to stand empty-handed, like he had been somehow tricked. His big sad hairy head, his facial shrug of embarrassment. What would the card even be for? Christmas was so long ago. Chinese New Year was so long ago. There has been nothing to say congratulations about for so long.

I am still gazing at the cards when the text comes in to say that Dad has found a place to park, there's a picture of where he is, and he's asking, *Am I in the right place?*

I reply, *Ha - No, you're not! But don't worry. There is actually a really nice place near where you are. It's recently been refurbished in fact and I'd like to see inside, because they have taken over two other whole restaurants that used to be next door, so it's absolutely enormous now! I want to see how big it is inside!*

Why do I always send him such long texts? Also, I really am not at all interested in how big this place will be inside. I don't know what happens to me, at all, when I have to see him.

OK, sounds fab, he texts.

Just stay there, I'll be two ticks, I reply.

So that's how I find him, sitting in his car, secretly smoking a cigarette.

'Hello my boy,' he says, and I am all at once squished into a hug with him, half-in and half-out of his car, his sweet-smelling jumper, and his husky corduroys, and the bitter smell he has these days.

We finish the lovely hug and I help him the rest of the way out of the car, which he doesn't need. He puts out his cigarette and gives me a guilty look.

'You're allowed to smoke, I don't care.'

'I know but...'

'Seriously, it's fine.'

I say, 'It's been too long, Dad!' I sound like I'm talking to a client.

'I know. I don't come often enough.'

'That's OK, normally I'm so busy, but the kids are in

school all day, and we can just catch up.'

'Of course, you can always come to me whenever you like,' he says. As always, I politely ignore this offer, and pretend I haven't heard what he's said.

Then I'm telling him all about the beer and the amount of food, and yes, the sheer unbelievable scale of this new mega-Turkish restaurant.

'I like Turkish food.'

'Not like this, Dad! You don't even know, Dad. You haven't even *eaten* Turkish food yet. You know, this stretch of road, this is basically the best place to eat if you like Turkish food, probably in the whole of the UK. Probably in most of Europe.'

And he's telling me about the diaspora in Germany, that probably Berlin has something similar. I ask if he's ever been to Berlin, and even while he is answering me, telling me about when he lived in West Berlin, I decide that he is telling me a lie.

I fling the door open to cut him off.

'Hello! Hey man!' I say to the waiter.

I recognise him from the last time I was here – before the refurbishment – but he does not recognise me, and does not respond to my friendly greeting. The waiter seems aloof, actually. Not at all the friendly guy who served me before. Thousands of people eat here every week, I guess, but I still feel a bit crestfallen. Dad doesn't seem to have noticed. He's standing right in the doorway, like an uncertain eagle, blocking the open door, sucking all the heat out into the street.

'Come in, Dad,' I say.

The waiter leads us to a table in the old part of the restaurant, the original bit before the extension happened.

'Wow,' I say, 'the place looks great! It's huge!' I'm saying it like this because I want him to know that I know what it was like before, that I'm not just some tourist.

The waiter is smiling and nodding. 'Yes, we recently had a refurbishment.'

'It looks fab,' Dad says in a shy voice.

I peer around the corner, and all I can see is more and more opulent Turkish restaurant. It's about half full. Through the angles I can see into what would once have been a different restaurant. There is an exposed brickwork arch leading through what used to be a wall, and beyond that, yet another arch.

'It basically goes down the street!' I say to Dad.

He nods and smiles.

We're drinking. A bottle of Efes beer each.

'So, Dad, I think we should get just this kebab to share, and some mezze. It will be so much food.'

'Sounds good. I like sharing.'

'Great!'

'This is nice!'

'Yes!'

While we wait for the food we talk about politics, and we tell each other facts. I ask him to remember some things for me, about when I was a child. It's a strange habit of mine, and possibly exhausting for him to have to remember all those years ago. I, myself can remember virtually nothing – not from childhood or from, for example, any job I had in the last five years. No useful details anyway. No stories unless they are highly insulting tales of the managers I have had.

Dad clears his throat, which makes him cough. He

coughs and coughs. I give him water and say, 'God, Dad, are you OK?'

He brokenly tells me he is fine.

'Your face is very pale, are you sure you're OK?'

'I'm fine,' he says, loudly clearing his throat again. 'I'm fine,' he says calmly and with a smile.

He tells me a story I'm not at all sure about, about a toy boat I had. We took it to the reservoir, he told me. Do you remember the reservoir?

'I do,' I say. 'Wow, it was such a weird place.'

'It was a weird place.'

'Yeah, but in my memory, Dad – you've no idea. It's like an alien landscape! The reservoir!'

'That's right.'

'Wow. And I had a boat? I think I remember. A blue boat with a sail?'

'That's right, blue and white boat.'

'And I got it from Aunt Eleanor?'

'Uncle Jim and Aunt Eleanor, yes. It would have been Jim's idea.'

'He was such a funny man.'

'Yes.'

'He used to hang me upside down.'

'That's right!'

The beer is making my lips buzz after not even half a bottle, and we talk some more about how strange things were, and the houses we have both lived in. We compare half-formed memories of these places, describing them to each other, possibly lying to each other, but it hardly seems to matter. Somewhere in the back of my mind, I think, this is just how we are – nothing is real. Our memories are just these delicate little lies. Mundane stories that only slightly vary from the surely equally mundane realities. I have that thought, but only very quietly. I am happy to be talking with Dad.

'We're terrible at describing these places,' I say.

'I think we're good at it.'

'We're terrible! We would make terrible architects, Dad!'

'Oh, I think you could be an architect if you want.'

'No. I'm thirty-five. I can't be an architect now.'

He shrugs.

We are still on the subject of places we have lived and I accidentally, but not really accidentally, bring up the time when he left. I know as I'm speaking that there are limits with him. There are things that even I am not allowed to say to him, even though I have more license than most. I do actually have the power to hurt him. But still...

'There was that time, wasn't there? When you first went. How long did you stay in that bedsit?'

'What?'

'That bedsit. You left us and went to live in a bedsit. Before you moved into that place with Jenny.'

'Hmm.'

'The bedsit, Dad. We were never allowed to come there. The bedsit!'

The food arrives just as I say the word bedsit again, and he's looking at me smiling, as if I haven't said anything. He is deaf, sometimes. He looks like a deaf old bird. Or a wolf.

He's a combination of animals really. His bear's eyes are really staring quite intently at me, but strangely low. Strangely at my chest, or my throat.

'This smells delicious!' I say to the waiter.

'Really fab!' Dad says, holding his hands out around his plate, as if it's a shock – this is so much food!

I smile at him, and he smiles at me and I ask the waiter for some more bread, maybe, I love the bread so much.

We start eating and I don't mention the bedsit again.

'Do you want to have another drink?' I ask him when the waiter comes by.

He looks at his glass, and he looks at the time. Inside himself, he probably looks at his letter from the DVLA confirming his twelve-month ban for drink driving in 2010.

'We could share one, Dad? What do you think?'

'Sure.'

So we get another beer and I pour out half each into our glasses. I also ask for the bill, and I pay with my card, but let Dad give me more than his share of it in cash.

'Take it, take it,' he is saying. He waves notes around, and I know he has taken out more than he can afford, saying take it, take it.

'No, no, no,' I say and I drink beer and he drinks beer and we clink our glasses together.

We sit for a while, in the aftermath of the food. He tells me about his work, he is trying to recruit someone for a managerial role. He tells me he is currently filling in, but he's an old hand, he says. They need someone with some energy. New ideas.

'I want to stop,' he says. 'But – the money is welcome.'

'Do you still have that hole in the ceiling?'

'Still there.'

He's got this hole in the ceiling, and the washing machine is resting very close to the hole. For some reason the washing machine is on the landing on top of this hole. Like he wants it to fall on his head!

'I really worry about that washing machine, Dad.'

'It's on a beam,' he tells me. 'It's completely safe.'

'I'm just going to the toilet,' I say.

The new bathrooms in the restaurant are very luxurious. Each cubicle has its own sink and floor length doors – like a proper room, not a cubicle at all. I have a long sitting-down wee and browse things on my phone, but the batteries start to go, and I remember Dad is out there.

I wash my hands, but the soap is so nice I want to wash them again. Then I am just letting warm water run and run over my hands. There's my face in the vast Rococo mirror. My chubby face, swollen instantly on all that bread and heat and one-and-a-half bottles of Efes.

A blue boat on the reservoir! I feel sure the whole thing is a fiction, but I remember grass, and a large white water silo. I remember walking a long way, and a barbed wire fence, and a low mist, and our dog, and my Dad's red cigarette tip, and the sound of hobby aircraft.

He used to love the idea of those hobby aircraft. He loved it so much, and we used to share a dream of one day buying one and flying it. We'll save up, we said, but of course it was impossible. There was never any saving. There was only the absolute dregs of credit card credit, and 10p crisps, and 'you'll have to share all of those things with your brother and sister.'

Which, obviously, is fine.

But, in this luxurious private room, in this lovely drowsy warm water warm air warm clothes warm cold sun – all that seems so long ago.

I have to get out of here. But there, in the corner of the mirror, there is a disturbing shape. The shape seems to move, but the light in this cubicle is quite slow-moving, and fuggy. The shape disturbs me a great deal, though I cannot describe it. It does not follow any formal proper-ties of an ordinary shape. What is it?

How long have I been standing here looking at it?

I rub my eyes, really stupidly hard, then lean into the mirror, touching the cold glass with my nose. On closer inspection, I find that the shape is nothing more than the coat hook on the door behind me.

When I finally get back to the table, my coat is still on the back of my chair, but my father is nowhere to be seen. Our food has been cleared away. All the people I remember seeing while I was eating have also gone: the couple I could see by the door; the work party of mostly men who were from the estate agent up the road. They've all gone. The restaurant is deserted.

I try to find the waiter who served us, but he is nowhere to be seen. I wonder if perhaps I am in the wrong part of the restaurant. It is huge after all, with all these different areas.

And yet – here is my coat. I check to make sure it is in fact my coat. But perhaps someone mistakenly picked it up and carried it a few steps, realised it wasn't theirs, and dumped it quickly on the back of this chair here, before hurrying back to find their own coat.

I find a waiter at last, but not the one who originally served us. He is cleaning an area of the floor with a mop. There is a lot of rice on the floor, a baby might have been sitting there. This is a good restaurant for families.

'Excuse me,' I'm saying, in quite a high-pitched panicky voice. 'Sorry to interrupt. I was here with my father. I mean, I am. I am here with him. I just nipped to the toilet, and when I came back all I could find was my coat. I think he might have got lost in your huge restaurant.'

The new waiter looked at me. 'I'm sorry,' he said. 'You lost your coat?' He asks me this looking directly at the coat I am holding in my hands.

'No – my father! He was sitting just here.' I feel queasy. The Efes. The coffee. The fucking blue sailing boat.

'Where are the other toilets? He must have gone to the wrong toilets or something.'

'Toilets are over there,' the waiter says, pointing over my shoulder, back in the direction I have just come from. His smile is looking fixed on now.

'But that's where I just came from,' I say.

The waiter shrugs.

'Oh, forget it. Don't worry. Sorry. He must be having a cigarette!' I say, and I go grumpily to the main entrance to peer out into the street. It's darkening, a cold late afternoon.

There is no sign of my father on the street. I close the door and turn back to the waiter.

'We were sitting just over there!' I say, getting desperate now. 'He wouldn't have left without at least telling some-one. Or leaving me a message. Did he leave me a message, do you know? Gone to move the car? Something like that?'

The waiter just apologises again, for not knowing. For having to get on. 'We get very busy in the evenings,' he tells me, 'lots of families will be coming here, very busy, a lot to prepare.'

'Look, I really need to see my father,' I say. 'I'll just wait here. He must have gone to check his ticket or something. He'll come back. I was just in the bathroom for a minute.'

'I'm sorry, but we are closed now.'

'Closed?'

'Yes, we close to get ready for the evening.'

'But I can wait here, can't I? I haven't finished my meal.'

'Sorry, but we are closed to the public, you can't be here.'

I point at the only table I can see with people still sitting and eating. 'But what about them? They're still eating? If they can stay then, surely... oh, I see, they work here.'

'Yes, they were working the lunch shift, now they have some food, and then back to work. Sorry.'

There is a temporary stand-off between me and the waiter, which I lose and go skulking out of the door. I walk up and down the street. Dad's car is not where I remember it being, but then I can't be exactly sure where it was. It is getting so dark, so absurdly dark.

He must have left. I call his number a few times, it goes straight to voicemail. I text him. *Where did you go?* He doesn't reply, which makes sense since he's not picking up when I call. A bit desperately, I text, *Is it because I did something wrong?* Then, cross with myself for asking such a babyish question, I text, *Well, I had a great time. Let's do it again soon.* Then I head home.

I get in and find the kids already in their pyjamas. My partner looks exhausted. I try to explain where I have been, but it's no good. I do the washing up. I clean the mess from dinner and bedtime. I make something for my partner to eat.

After an hour, I find myself in my son's room. I give him a little kiss on his sleeping head. I go to my daughter's room and give her a little kiss on her head.

Am I draining something from them, I wonder? Am I taking their goodness away? I often wonder these stupid things. I promise them I will never lie about their childhood. If I can't remember anything, then all I can tell them is the truth – I loved you and I worried a lot about a great many things.

'I'm going to go and try to find him,' I tell my partner.

She tells me there's no point.

'I know,' I say, even as I zip up my coat and open the front door. 'I know there's no point. I'll be back soon I expect. I'm sorry.'

She is accustomed to my somewhat unpredictable behaviour where meetings with Dad are concerned. As usual, her goodbye is warm and kind – even when we fight bitterly, we manage as nice a goodbye as we possibly can.

The restaurant is in complete darkness. The place is so cavernous, it's impossible to tell if there is anyone inside at all. I rattle the doors. Nobody responds. There are no signs of life whatsoever.

A young man in a trench coat walking past looks at me quizzically.

'Do you know if they're open?' I ask him.

'Sorry mate,' he says, then continues past.

I keep stupidly peering into the darkness of the restaurant. All the other places are open. Smoke from their barbecues wafts down the street.

I see a glimpse of something moving about inside. It looks not human, but perhaps like an animal. It gives me that rat-shiver I get whenever I see rodents in the bushes in the parks. A sense that I am dirty. I see it again, and realise it is not a rat, but the movement of people's feet on the pavement, reflected on a surface, somewhere inside the restaurant.

I walk down the street a little way, and discover the restaurant has a second entrance. A small, hand-written sign says: *CLOSED. VERY SORRY. OPEN TOMORROW.*

When I turn away from the sign in disgust, I notice Dad's car, sitting on the other side of the street.

I dash across the road, running towards his car. It's not

forty metres from where he originally was when I found him before lunch. It is parked at a funny angle, as though he may have dumped it here and scuttled off in urgent need of a ticket machine, a toilet, or cigarettes. I cup my hands around my eyes and look in through the passenger window. He isn't in there. It's just the usual mess of coffee cups and broken cassette boxes, dust and fluff speckles the black floor carpets, the ashtray is flopped guiltily open with a couple of skinny rollie stubs peeping out, reminding him to throw them away before anyone who cares about his health sees them.

The back seat is a strange and different story. Nestled in amongst Dad's crap coat and bag, there are other things, more precious objects. A lot of pictures, lovingly framed lie on the red leather seats. Photographs of different people I recognise as friends of my Dad's from his school days. There are photos of comedian Kenny Everett and Tony Slattery and Stephen Fry, who he worked with on different teaching projects in which actors and comedians sometimes took part. There's also Bernard, a frightening mechanic friend of his who, I strangely remember, lived in a garage on a camp bed from the war. There are a few men with thick black facial hair, smiling in their Morris Dancer clothes.

There is my reflection, all lines and dark hollows. Tired and stressed.

Then I hear Dad's voice behind me – firmer than before, tighter, younger. 'Get in then,' he says.

I look up and see him standing there, opening the passenger door.

'Dad! Where have you been? I was so worried! Didn't you get my texts? Where have you been?'

He smiles and shakes his head slowly. He is

infuriatingly passive and calm, seeming to enjoy the bite of cold on the night air. He looks thinner too. 'You haven't noticed have you?' he says.

'Noticed what? Where did you go, Dad? Where the fuck have you been, actually?'

'You keep asking that. Look at the car.'

'It's your old car,' I say, recognising it as I spoke. 'But you destroyed your one. The accident you had. Where did you find this one?'

'Not completely destroyed, after all. Uncle Paul fixed it up. You remember uncle Paul? My uncle Paul, that is.'

'I do. I think so. Tall?'

'That's right. Tall Paul.'

Dad keeps his eyes on me, watching me remember Tall Paul, an ancient man I never think about, but can now picture in great detail, a bald head with stern white wisps across it. A sort of dour mouth that could lift easily into a heartening grin. Tall, of course, a giant with startling blue eyes.

'Didn't he have a lisp?' I ask.

'That's right!'

'He was a bit odd. Didn't he die though?'

'Heart attack, but he fixed the car up for me long before then.'

'So. But that must have been twenty-five years.'

'That's right.'

'But it looks, I mean, it looks exactly the same.'

'Storage,' is all he says about the car's fabulous condition. 'Get in, eh? A quick drive.'

And now I am in the car with him, we've been travelling for a while, and I feel vague. 'Dad – I need to get home. They'll be wondering.'

'You used to love falling asleep in this car,' he says.

'Yes, did I?'

'You used to love falling asleep in the front seat. You liked the arm rests.'

'It's true!' I say. 'I used to come out and get into the car and wait for you, for ages. Just wait in the front seat. Sometimes I knew you would come out, and other times I knew you wouldn't, but I still came out and waited.'

'That's right. You didn't listen when we said there was nowhere to go. You'd get into this kind of mood and go out there and sit and sit for hours.'

I'm curled up in the front seat, and Dad's telling me, unbidden, more about Tall Paul. This guy who I barely even remember. Who I scarcely credit as having existed at all, is now a major figure in our past.

Dad is telling the story of the time he and Uncle Paul rescued the farmer's dog once. He's explaining something about it getting lost in the neighbouring small holding. Small holding is something I have asked twice for the meaning of, but Dad's words slip and drift under the car. We have been driving for perhaps three hours. I think of home, my children. I think of the ache of being apart from them. I smile – but small holdings. Small holdings, and then I am sleeping.

Dad tells me I slept the whole time. 'We got lost.' He laughs. 'And you didn't even notice.' He laughs again at that, and some spit comes out of his mouth. I find it repulsive, and yet, I like it. I can smell his jumper. Vanilla tobacco, that is the smell of his spit, like jasmine almost. The old smell. He tells me he ate an entire meal in the Little Chef and I stayed asleep in the car.

'You are so tired,' he tells me. 'You are so, so tired.' And he looks very sad.

I tell him I recognise the roads as we cruise down from the dual carriageway, into the provincial back-lanes of the town of my childhood.

'You really want to see it, don't you?' Dad asks me.

'I really do,' I say, even though I'm too groggy to really know what he means. I am agreeing to please him. I feel so pleasantly drowsy.

'I thought you'd forgotten about that bedsit,' Dad says.

'No, I never did.'

'But you never came to it. Too depressing. Oh, I could not have born it.'

'Neither could Mum. She wouldn't let us ask you about it.'

'That's right. We agreed not to mention the bedsit.'

'I asked you to explain over and over again what a bedsit actually is.'

'That's right.'

The car sloops through cul-de-sacs and avenues. I become excited when we reach Oakdale – a tree-lined lane with long front lawns that unfold into slack, wide semi-detached homes. I feel heartened by the promise of this mizzled early morning. I tell myself that my partner will be furious, and worried frantic, but that it will be forgiven. In time, this will be forgiven. I will make it up to her. There will come a moment in her life, like this one in mine, when she has to endure some kind of inexplicable situation with her parents. I feel convinced of this inevitable moment in the future, when my partner will vanish for a night or two without explaining why, and I will have the kids, and I will definitely understand, and I will ask no questions.

I am glad it is the autumn. The autumn is when things happen in this town. The summer is droopy and the people become obvious and beery and numb. Winter is brittle and spring is too short and wet. But the autumn is full of action and weirdness as new term begins in the schools, and new kids emerge from the woodwork, and new students start shifts in the pubs.

I am heartened by seeing the dog-walkers. I wave to their unseeing backs.

A gang of kids wind by, two on bikes and two walking. The bikers snake slowly to keep time with their ambling friends. I watch them, knowing the action, the tension of the handlebars, the boredom of what lies in wait. I am sorry when we pass them, leaving them to make their way up and over the Roach Road bridge.

We turn and turn. We hit the centre, and travel up through the high street, chugging at each pedestrian crossing while people traverse at their leisure, unhurried by Dad's growling white car.

I peer into Willmotts, Dillons, Budgens, Craft Wools. I notice the prominent St George flags outside the pubs. Not all of the pubs have them, but most do. 'I hate those flags,' I say.

'Awful,' Dad says, but he hasn't looked at them, his focus is entirely on the road.

I look at myself in the little vanity mirror on the sun-shade. Behind me, in the distance, is Quarry Lane, which lies beneath an arch of faded, crumbling trees. The scattered branches are like eyelashes against the white skin of the sky.

Also, I notice that my facial hair is helping my jawline more than I thought it was this morning. I lift my chin. Really not bad at all. Maybe because I skipped breakfast with Dad in the Little Chef? I have a strong chin, from certain angles. The mirror snaps shut. My father is muttering something entirely to himself about vanity.

'What was that for?' I demand, with a nervous little bit of laughter in my voice. I open the mirror again and resume my inspection. He snaps it back and I open it again. The car swerves very slightly.

I ask him, 'Are you really going to crash this car for the sake of me looking in the mirror?'

He doesn't answer.

'Are you, Dad? Are you really going to drive this shitty fucking car into a lamppost because I am using the mirror?' I said, 'Are you really going to kill us both? What a good idea! There!' I'm shouting, 'There's the British Legion! Let's do it there. Come on,' I'm shouting, 'let's go through the wall of the British Legion, like kamikaze warriors!'

I slip my right arm towards the steering wheel, but before I can touch it, Dad slams on the brakes and we are both thrown forward, into the old fashioned, unforgiving safety belts. My neck hurts.

'A dog!' Dad shouts at me.

In front of us, a shabby-looking spaniel, all on its own, is crossing the road.

'Do you think we should go and check it's OK?'

'It's fine,' he says. 'Someone will find it. Lucky not to have been killed.'

We pull away gently, and glide over the hill. We are heading towards the industrial part of town where the old landfill site is, a few warehouses, a small timber yard. I have been there a couple of times.

'Are we nearly there, then?' I ask, though I am not expecting a reply after our little altercation about the mirror.

'Hmm,' Dad says.

'Are we at the end of our mysterious adventure, Dad? I've left my family behind for this,' I say. 'I'm paying a price for this. So, the least you can do is tell me if we're there or not.'

'Yes,' he says. 'Yes, we are here.' He is smiling somewhat wolfishly. 'Now we are here. Wait in the car.'

He gets out and I watch him approach an imposing Edwardian terraced house with a large black door. He looks like he's going towards the bin area. There are six wheelie bins in an alley between the ground floor of this house and the one next door. I see him talking to someone, a large blond man. It looks like the man and my Dad are arguing.

The argument looks serious, and the large, rat-blond man looks very aggressive. I worry about Dad's collapsible lung. He's had three collapsed lung emergencies. He's not a well man. I wonder if I should get out of the car, but I am paralysed with fear. The big blond man is in fact Mick Pollard. Mick Pollard who I went to school with. Mick Pollard, my bully. I am paralysed with fear.

Dad is tossing his head back and laughing at Mick Pollard, but he shouldn't do that. Mick Pollard has a dreadful temper. Everyone knows about it. Suddenly, Dad cuts out of the argument and runs towards the front door of the terraced Edwardian house, sorting through keys as he goes. Mick Pollard flaps an irritated hand at him and stalks away down the road with his phone pressed hard against his ear.

When Mick has gone, I take a deep breath, get out of the car and run towards Dad.

'Come on,' Dad says, letting me into the side entrance of the house.

'Why are you arguing with Mick Pollard?' I say.

'Never mind him – up the stairs quick!' Dad says.

He shoves me in the back, and I start climbing these

spongey, foul-carpeted stairs. I ask Dad again about Mick Pollard.

'He's the freeholder,' Dad says, close behind me, his voice breathy with the climb. 'He wants to buy the bedsit, but I won't let him. Silly fat bastard!'

Dad laughs at himself calling Mick Pollard a silly fat bastard. We keep climbing, and I worry about Dad's lung, but he seems to be coping with the stairs better than me. My heart's pounding already.

We reach a window and I see the alley down below. Mick Pollard is on the phone, looking furious.

'Quick!' Dad says, barging me away from the window. 'Up! We have to go up!'

We are on the second floor already, and the communal areas and the stairwell have opened out into something altogether more lavish. There are exquisite table lamps, and expensive Persian rugs, and an array of exquisite Japanese paintings, or at least paintings inspired by Japanese art of the eighteenth century.

The stairs and bannister are polished oak, with a charcoal sisal runner. The walls are 'Downpipe' by Farrow and Ball.

'This place is amazing.'

Dad nods. 'That's right,' he says – though he can barely talk. His lung is definitely collapsing, I think. At least one of them is, but he is smiling. He looks so young and scurrilous suddenly.

We go up, and leave this luxury behind. As we rise, the style becomes more and more faded. Without Dad having to tell me, I know that his bedsit will be in the very top of this house. We have climbed seven floors already, and there are more to go as the bannister spirals in ever- smaller, ever-tattier circles. The air is becoming damp. The portraits on the walls are smaller, with faded – even gruesome – faces.

A portrait of Sir Walter Scott is grizzled and his thin red lips droop in a disturbing way. His eyes are black and much too big for his face.

'This portrait of Sir Walter Scott smells of rotten fish, Dad,' I say.

'That's right,' he wheezes.

We finally reach the highest point of the house. A door of faded mint green, with a turtle-shell Bakelite knob and a large iron keyhole. Dad fishes out a hefty, teeming bunch of keys, folding them carefully over until he finds the right one. Down below, I hear the crashing of Mick Pollard. He is not alone. Male voices come screaming and booming up the stairs.

'Are you sure he just wants to buy the bedsit, Dad? He sounds angry.'

'He's always angry. Silly fucker.'

Dad laughs again at his insulting disregard for the man who used to bully me at school.

'Dad, he's got people with him.'

'Don't worry. He can't get in without a key.'

We are inside the bedsit.

I try to take it all in while Dad shoves an arm chair up against the door. The cramped space is divided by a series of yellowing paisley curtains. Kitchenette area over by the window, blurred by white paint. Sleeping area is a bedframe with no mattress, set back from the shoreline of the kitchen lino. In the corner, a crumbling rose-coloured toilet peeps from behind a ply-wood door.

Dad finishes the barricade and rushes to join me in the kitchenette. He pulls out the bottom drawer of the free-standing kitchen unit and empties it onto the sideboard. A hammer and a few odd keys fell out.

He picks up the hammer and lunges at the wall beside me.

'Stand back,' he says, and then he starts smashing at the wall with the hammer.

'Dad? What are you doing?'

'You'll see!' He says. The wall seems to give way beneath his hammer-blows surprisingly easily. I watch him, hammering for about four or five minutes until finally, his energy seems to fall away.

He breathes my name as he collapses, stumbles back. 'I– I–' He says, and he's gulping like a fish. 'I can't anymore. You carry on.'

'But what am I doing?' I beg him. I beg him to tell me what any of this means.

'Quickly,' he says. 'If they manage to get through that door, you have no idea. You just have no idea.'

I start bashing away at the wall, just like he did, but all my strength seems to have gone. My months of going to the gym. I'm jelly. I am awful.

'Fuckssake,' Dad growls. He growls the way I growl at my son, the way he growled at me when he still lived with us, the way my mother too, from time to time, is known to growl. He reaches up and claws at the ruined plaster with his fingers. As chunks of damp white plaster come away, I see something in the wall. A sliver of metal. A half-brick tumbles away. He rakes at it. I try to help him. We keep pulling at the bricks. They come away easily now from the flaking mortar – the sting of my fingernails tearing fades instantly to numbness.

A blue metallic outline, a rim of something, about the width of an old twelve-inch television, a glass something.

'It's there!' Dad says. 'Hurry!'

The men are here. They are pounding on the door now. Their voices. There's the voice of Mick Pollard. He's furious. He's saying horrible things. He's going to shit down my neck, he is saying, he is breathing and booming on the door, the speed of his pounding is impressive. He's a piston. He's a killer. He paralyses me. I–

'Ignore him,' Dad says. 'Just keep going. Put your back into it.'

So I do, I keep shanking away at the bricks. My fingers are bleeding, but I feel this strange rush of something. Like a happiness? This happiness, my Dad has his hand on my back, at the very bottom of my back, the small-holding of my back. Before long, I burst through into a tiny cave in the wall. There is something there, in the recess.

'I've done it!' I shout.

Gasping, Dad pulls himself up onto his feet and together we ease out this small oven. This Mondelux single-man-in-a-bedsit oven with rotisserie setting and three other different functions.

'Very, very careful,' he says. 'Don't break the cords.'

As I look behind the oven, I see that it is attached to the wall by a rope of thin steel wires, bunched together to make a thick... root... is the only word for it.

'Here,' Dad says to me, holding the oven on his own. 'Open the door.'

I pull the oven door and it opens in this smooth, greasy way.

'What can you see?' he says. 'Look, look right inside.'

'I can see a lane, a cobwebbed tunnel, leading into a dark cave. I can see a house encased in ivy. I can see–'

'Look closer.'

'I see the foggy, drooping eye socket of Sir Walter Scott.'

'Look closer.'

'I can see Steven Fry holding a basket of dust.'

'Look closer.'

'I can see. Wait! I can see colours. I can see beautiful red, with a white stripe along it, and a sail. A small, perfectly formed sail. But I thought it was blue.'

'That's right.'

'I can see my hand.'

'Go right inside.'

'I can see my ludicrous, tiny, pink hand, and the reservoir. I can see it all. But what about everything else?'

'Go all the way inside the oven, he says.'

'No, I don't think... I don't think I want...'

I turn back, and Dad is smiling very kindly. He is peaceful-looking and pale grey.

'Go all the way inside the oven,' he says to me again. 'If you go all the way inside the oven, you can have the little boat.'

'I don't want to go into the oven, Dad. I've got a family. I've got the wet washing to worry about.'

He's tapping me, lightly, on the back.

'Get into the oven, darling boy, get into the oven and you can try again, you can have another go with the little boat.'

ALL SILKY AND WONDERFUL

I finished reading the message just as the train entered the tunnel. There was that blast of noise as the windows blew open and the carriage filled with the roaring of confused, displaced air. The lights flickered out, leaving us lit by emergency signs. Not for the first time with this tunnel, I wondered if we had actually slammed into the wall this time. I looked at the grey skin light of my hands and asked myself, 'Am I floating in space?'

I looked around at my fellow passengers, as though they might reflect my own feelings about the tunnel. Had we entered a new kind of space? Were we still physical things? They were looking down at their phones, of course. There was no indication from them that we had lost physical form.

I turned back to my own phone and reread the terrible news. The message had been sent to me more than a month ago and had been sitting in that unchecked inbox all this time. News of a death should not be ignored like that. Now that I'd opened the message, they would know. A reply was urgently needed.

My attempted consolations were treacherous. It was easy enough to remember my friend, or rather, the girl I had known at school. I could see her looking quizzical in a French lesson, or adoring satsumas in the common room. The charismatic girl who had always laughed with her whole hand over her face, who had understood perfectly the simple pleasures of walking around the corridors, seeing friends, engaging with everything all at once. I could see her, but what I wrote was horribly formless. These big, goofy memories that were all about me.

I'm in a tunnel, I wrote at one point. *I wish that I could emerge from it in the past and see her again. I would make more of an effort to be a real friend to her. We lost touch, you see, after school. I have no idea how long I've been in here, in the dark. I have no scale, no sense of time. I feel a contortion in my physical form, which might even be a connection to her, here in the void. In this space my memories are more than memories. I can see her again. I can sense her charisma, her generosity–*

I had to delete all of it, obviously. The tunnel ended, and I cut my message back to: *I am thinking of you all*, followed by a curt paragraph break. *I will drink a toast and remember her. X*

I closed my eyes. Tried not to chastise myself for being so banal.

I came out of a brief doze to discover that my carriage was now completely empty. I hadn't noticed anyone leaving, but then I had been asleep.

For a moment I panicked. Had I missed my stop? I started feverishly gathering my things together, but then I saw that Big Andrew's belongings were still draped across his table. Big Andrew always took that table and made sure the whole space was dominated by his expressive teal leather luggage. Big Andrew's stop was before mine; watching him shout 'bugger' at the doors as he tried to shove his way through was a regular cue for me to start mentally preparing myself to get off the train.

I felt relieved. But then I remembered that my friend was no longer alive. Then I remembered my feeble condolence message. Then I remembered I had to run a workshop later. I thought of my workplace, and the situation with my performance lately. I thought about how my feelings on this journey into work would be considered to be yet another case of me 'thinking too much'.

Then I thought of Big Andrew, whose loud, sulky voice interrupted my thoughts. I looked around but I couldn't see him. 'Cut it loose,' Big Andrew was saying. 'Cut it loose, I can't stand it. I can't bear it. I won't abide those things. Something has happened. Something has happened.'

His voice was extraordinary. I'd heard Big Andrew talking on his phone many times before – he was a regular phone shouter on this journey – but now he sounded as if he was in pain. Or like he needed the toilet. Like he was being tortured and needed a piss.

Another voice responded to him, tried to soothe Big panicky Andrew. I could not exactly hear what this soother was saying, but it was a deep, placating voice. A voice that worked for the train company.

I got out of my chair and turned to look for Big Andrew, scanning the empty carriage as his disembodied voice wailed on unseen. 'Cut it loose, please God, cut it loose.'

At last, I saw him. He was only just visible behind a small crowd gathered at the internal doorway, just inside the next carriage. He was sort of crouching behind people, biting his bottom lip, his eyes staring wildly into the carriage in which I now stood alone.

Imagine a man. He would've captained the rugby team – a kind, deep-voiced man. Imagine that man in his car. A very expensive but practical model with a roof rack for bikes. He's gracefully greyed. He's married. He has the same friends he's had since he was in his teens. Imagine this man. He's had maybe one cautious, short affair but that's in the past. Recently, he's switched up his wardrobe. He travels in the carriage he likes, whether or not it's First Class. You have just imagined Big Andrew.

And there he was cowering behind a crowd of people who were tiny by comparison. People who were, until very recently, sitting in my carriage.

Quite self-consciously, and with a vague sense that the rear carriage must have been evacuated for some reason, I stowed my phone, grabbed my bag and my jacket and headed towards them.

As I was about to cross over the threshold into the next carriage, the guard appeared, stopping my progress. He seemed to be putting himself between me and Big Andrew specifically, keeping me in that ribbed, snaky corridor thing that connected the two carriages. I could feel my feet being manipulated, rising and falling, tipping and pointing as he spoke to me.

'Sorry, you can't come through,' the guard said. He was young, and had a puffy mid-twenties face, with patches of mid-length stubble. I ignored his words and continued forward. The guard didn't move, however, so I ended up pressing against him. Our chests and, because of a jolt in the train's movement, the tops of our thighs touched. We both grunted in an undignified way.

'All right,' I said, backing away, trying to show I wasn't going to force my way through.

'You can't come through. Just stay there,' the guard said, holding out his hand, palm towards me. He actually seemed very flustered.

'What's wrong?' I said, trying to bring an amused inflection into my voice. 'Why has everyone else left the carriage? Why can't I come through?'

'There's a situation we are reviewing at the moment,' the guard said. He was leaning against the doorway. He seemed to be doing something with his right arm, which I could not see. At first, I assumed he was steadying himself in an attempt to exude an air of authority and stillness. But then I wondered if there was some kind of weapon or control panel concealed where his arm was.

He seemed to have finished speaking – as though no futher explanation was necessary. Was he waiting for me to attack?

I had the rising sense of being trapped, the flood of adrenaline weakened my voice. When I tried to protest, I sounded like a leaflet about an obscure man, unjustly alone in a train carriage. 'Tell me why I can't come through, please,' I said.

'I'm sorry,' was all the guard said. 'But there is an issue with this carriage.'

'What issue?' I asked, very softly.

'It's a difficult situation, I'm afraid. Very complicated. There are certain objects in the carriage which are causing problems for us.'

'What objects?'

'Specifically, those bags.' The guard gestured with a flat-handed chop towards Big Andrew's luggage.

'But those bags are his!' I said, pointing at Big Andrew. He bit his lip as our eyes met, then he recoiled, dipping between the shoulders of a couple of other passengers. It was as if he was afraid of me.

'Andrew!' I said. 'Mate! Tell him they're nothing to do with me.'

Big Andrew whispered into the guard's ear, assuring him that we did not know each other. That he was shocked to hear I knew his name.

The guard spoke soothingly to Big Andrew before turning firmly back to me.

'Yes, the owner of the bags is the one who reported the problem. He says that he came into this carriage to talk on the phone. Leaving his bags in that carriage, the rear carriage, with you.'

'He didn't leave them *with* me. He left them. You left them, mate, that's all.'

'All right then, he left them alone with you. When he returned, he saw that they had been altered. He felt unable to cross the threshold into that carriage –'

'Wait,' I said. 'I mean. Sorry, I've had a bit of bad news just now. What do you mean, altered? Andrew, what the fuck is going on?'

The guard and Big Andrew consulted again, and this time when the guard spoke to me he seemed more serious.

'What happened was he went away and returned to the threshold of the carriage and felt unable to cross into the rear carriage, because the bag, or bags, were in an altered state. He couldn't approach them at all. The entire space around them was altered.'

'But altered how? Like tampered with? Like a bomb? Oh Jesus, I don't need this! Is it a bomb?'

'No-no-no-no,' said the guard. 'No-no-no-no. Not a bomb. This is difficult to explain, but believe me, I think if you were on this side of the threshold you would see it more clearly.'

'So let me come over there then!' I demanded, but the guard, Big Andrew and various other gathered passengers steeled themselves against my approach.

It's hard to get across just how weak I was feeling. I had no fight in me at all. The adrenaline made me feel sick and shaky. Being in the rubbery threshold area wasn't helping. My legs were entirely at the mercy of the shifting space that controlled the ribbed corridor. The pressure coming from the void below was like a horrible and perverse foot massage. I was unable to gather any strength at all, and backed down at the faintest sign of opposition.

The guard, I was sure, realised he was in complete control of me. He continued in a serious, professional manner.

'Firstly, rest assured, your life does not appear to be in immediate danger. We simply have a feeling of immense concern regarding those bags. An existential feeling, it's called. Like, you could say it's a bit like radioactive decay. Something resonates in the bones when we look at those bags. I should urgently point out that we do not literally mean radioactive. We are not considering this to be a terrorist incident of any kind. But the bone-level sense of doom emanating from the bags, and from this carriage space generally, does mean we may have to decouple you.'

'Don't decouple me!' I said.

'We may have to,' the guard said. Then, he moved his

body in a barely perceptible way, setting himself more firmly in the doorway between our carriages, making his body into more of a physical structure – a hard frontier between the trustworthy, honest world behind him and the zone that I was in, with the bags and their negative isotopes. Behind him, the other passengers also set themselves against me. Their faces were subtly altered, as though they were now confronted with an unpleasant cleaning task – say, a dead and half-rotted pigeon, discovered behind a voided fireplace.

I felt sure that if I rushed them, they would turn themselves against me as a single body. They would grimace and groan as they collectively pushed me away. It would be a traumatic but necessary undertaking for them, to shove me away. I had no power against them.

Hopelessly, I resumed pleading with the guard, but I was incoherent, unconvincing, as though my language had been degraded by this emanation that everyone else could understand, but I could not.

When my voice finally found traction, the tone was well off. I had now adopted the pitch of the hopelessly condemned. 'Please don't decouple me!' I said. 'You don't understand – I've got to run a workshop. Eleven people have said they will attend! Please!'

'I'm sorry, no,' was all I got.

'Why? Just tell me why can't I leave the carriage? Why must my day, my job, my work – you understand? Why is that suddenly meaningless? Why is this happening? What is this? I mean – what the fuck?'

The guard sighed and shook his head, as though by saying 'fuck' a second time, I had condemned myself utterly. Any chance of escape was gone now.

'He persistently used abusive and foul language,' the guard would say to his superiors. 'Specifically, he said "fuck" multiple times. Unfortunately, that confirmed it for me: I had no option other than to decouple him.'

'You have been alone with the bags,' he said. 'And so you are now, perhaps unwittingly, connected to the bags. You might not be, but we can't take any risks.'

I was about to protest, to thrust myself forward, when Big Andrew popped up behind the guard, pointing in my direction.

'He stares at me!' he blurted. His voice full of spit. As he said it, a wave passed through the gathered crowd, as though they had received confirmation of some awful suspicion. Big Andrew grew bolder, he rose to his full height. 'Every time I get on this train, he stares at me! It's horrible. It's like he's assessing me. Like he's undressing me with his mind. It's perverse!'

'I don't undress you with my mind!' I said, but I didn't sound convincing. The truth is I did stare at Andrew. He was just so massive. He was physically fascinating. His ears, for example – those two fleshy, cauliflower ruins. I had stared at Andrew a lot. I had even pictured his naked body. In my defence, not that I'd be mentioning it, I had pictured it as an artist would: the garish colours of his private area; the hair in his cracks; the pocked creases of his expansive skin. I *had* stared at him – I couldn't deny it – but could harmlessly imagining someone's massive nude body really be punishable by a decoupling?

For a second, there was no change. We remained exactly as we were. All at once the reality of what was about to happen gripped. I pleaded with renewed vigour, trying to appeal to some sense of reason, staring into the guard's tired eyes.

'They're not my bags. I don't see why those bags have

any bearing on me. Why should I be blamed?'

The guard only shook his head, sadly. 'You're right. You're right. You haven't done anything wrong.'

As he spoke, I could see that he was doing something with his hidden arm, moving it up and down out of sight, while keeping his eyes firmly fixed on me.

There was an unsettling clunk.

'Step back,' the guard said, quite forcefully.

I obeyed.

The doors between the carriages closed. I was alone in the rubbery airlock.

The guard pointed to his right ear. I didn't understand at first, but then he started pressing his ear against the glass, looking at me to see if I had caught on.

'You want me to press my ear to the glass?' I said. 'Like this?' I moved my ear towards the glass.

'That's right,' he mouthed, nodding.

With my ear pressed against the glass, the guard's voice felt close, free from the jagged sounds of the train. It was as though we were in a small, still room together.

'Just stay in the carriage,' he said. 'The decoupling process has started. Stay calm, and you will be absolutely fine. It's actually a very peaceful process. A gradual slowing, then stopping, and then it's over.'

'You make it sound like I'm dying,' I said.

The guard acted as though I hadn't spoken. 'In a moment, I will ask you to return to your carriage. When that happens, take your seat, facing back towards the main body of the train. Whatever happens, remain seated. You will begin to slowly reduce speed. Gradually, your carriage will be unable to continue to move forwards. It's very important that you do not try to exit or move about at this time. The carriage will come to a stop, and then it will begin rolling back down the hill we are currently climbing. It will gradually accelerate, before losing momentum on the opposite incline. After some adjustment, some back and forth, you will come to a natural stop in the trough of the valley. At that point, you should wait for a member of staff to come and help you disembark from the carriage.'

I took my ear from the glass to shout a question at him, 'What if another train comes?'

'Oh, that's very unlikely.'

'But what if it does?'

'Listen, I appreciate this is all rather worrying, and you have been very cooperative. I will write to my line manager and ensure your understanding and patience are acknowledged. You said just now that you had received some bad news? Perhaps this would be a good moment to spend alone in quiet contemplation. The natural landscape at the trough of the valley is really superb. You may find it brings you perspective.'

'What if nobody comes?'

'Between you and me, we can't prevent you from leaving the carriage after it has stopped. You will be alone. You will be free to explore the surrounding area. I'm not saying anything about what you should do, but if you were to leave the carriage, and travel west on foot, you would find a road before long. You could go off. Take some time – who would blame you for that? Now, please take your seat. Goodbye.'

It went just as he said. There was a loud clunk, and immediately I felt a decrease in speed. Air rushed into the carriage. I saw the faces of Big Andrew and the other passengers gathered at the window of the now departing train. Their faces were unreadable.

They vanished from view as the rubber corridor that formed a gangway between the carriages fell away from the rest of the train. It drooped down, flopping languidly just above the tracks. It was hard to imagine that a few moments ago, I had been standing on that now-collapsed threshold. I watched the floppy corridor for a while, but as the speed of my carriage reduced, I decided to move about among the seats, in open rebellion against the guard's advice to remain seated. I felt like I was on a rollercoaster, being manoeuvred into position before a big dip.

I was surprised by how long it took for the carriage to stop moving uphill. A minute or so passed before it came to a stop. There was a moment of stillness, of absolute calm, and then came the descent.

Accelerating back down the hill, I took my seat. The carriage felt ghostly, totally uncontrolled. I tensed myself against an impact that never came. I felt the movement in the darkness of the tunnels as a series of serene clouds, darkening the journey almost in silence. No other train came. The air through the windows and the gaps around the connecting door was sweet and warm. I felt the rise and fall in my stomach, as a kind of expanding, luxurious sponge.

And if there was a collision waiting for me somewhere down the line, I embraced that feeling too. I thought about her again, about my friend. I tried to imagine her on a wonderful journey, rolling softly along.

I came gently to a halt in the trough of the valley, just as the guard had said I would. Outside there were lush-ly-coloured fields I did not recognise, even though I must have passed them every day on my way to work.

I'd often felt that there was a period on this journey

when I completely blacked out. Every day, after ten minutes or so of worrying about work, and another ten of drifting in and out of whatever I'm reading or listening to, I had a sense that something had passed me by, unnoticed.

Was this what I had been missing? These yellow fields, maybe flax? Lines and lines of little yellow flowers under a blue sky. I felt a strange energy, an urge to be out of the carriage and breathing that air. I gathered Big Andrew's bags together, along with my own rucksack and struggled to the exit. I hauled down the window, undid the latch, opened the door and climbed down. The road was just a few metres away from the train track. I had to nip across a deserted track to get to it. I stood on the road, and looked back at my carriage. It looked sad. The droopy concertina tunnel sagged at the front.

It was hard going with Big Andrew's luggage. Every time I dropped one or other of the smaller cases, I wondered why I was bothering to take it with me at all. Each time I looked at it on the floor, I thought, 'Fuck it – leave it there.' But then I was picking it all up again and struggling on. I stuck to the centre of the road, enjoying the sun on my back. I could hear birdsong. I could see a tree. I had no idea if I was heading in the right direction. I felt quietly uplifted by the whole thing of being on the road, burdened and a bit hot, but generally alright.

After about twenty-five minutes, coming over the crest of a smallish hill, I saw an unexpected building, a solid oblong with hard-cut windows and blue sky reflected on the glass. Its angular walls were painted fresh white. There was a sign by the roadside: HOTEL.

The hotel porter greeted me, I have to say, with

considerable professionalism. She did not seem surprised to find someone looking as bedraggled as I did, carrying quite unsuitable luggage for a foot journey, turning up at the hotel completely unprepared and without a reservation.

'I came from the road,' I said, gesturing behind me.

'Oh yes,' she said. 'Welcome.' She gestured to the luggage. 'Can I assist you with those bags?'

It was at that moment that I realised why I had been carrying Big Andrew's luggage. I laid them out in front of her, so she could get a good look.

'You're not afraid of or disgusted by these bags?' I asked.

'Ah, no?' she said. 'Not in the least. It looks like normal, fairly expensive luggage to me.'

'Yes,' I agreed. 'Just some bags, aren't they? Sorry, I know it's a strange way to introduce myself. Only there was a bit of an incident earlier. Some people felt that these bags were, ah, altered.'

The hotel porter just looked at me, smiling in a strong, carefree, youthful way. When she leaned in, seemingly to confide something, I was struck by the air around her. That cleanness that some people have, that naturally sweet and healthy breath.

'My experience,' she said, 'is that those feelings generally fade from an object once it has been removed from the context in which it became altered.' She said this matter-of-factly, as though bone-level emotionally disturbing objects were commonplace.

'Do guests often describe luggage in this way?' I asked.

'Sometimes.'

'Really? And. Ah, the ones that do – do they arrive by train? Or I should say, by train carriage?'

'Sometimes,' she said again. 'We get a few of you from the train tracks. But sometimes it's been in other settings altogether, not at the hotel. Not even at work at all. For example, in my house, there appeared a coat that none of us could abide. It ended up in the cupboard under the stairs after, I think, a party. Nobody knew whose it was. Nobody wanted to touch or wear that coat. But we weren't into throwing stuff away that had a use. Even a great big waxy thing like that. Well, I say great big and waxy, but really nobody could get across any true physical details of it. It just lay huddled there, under a few bags, giving off this terrible vibe.

'But then one day it was raining, and a house guest – I don't remember who, but one of us had a house guest – needed to get home in a hurry but had not expected rainfall. I said, "Fetch the waxy coat." Someone fetched it, and it turned out to be quite stylish actually. As soon as the guest put it on, that woeful feeling it had been giving off just went away. We were left looking at our guest wearing what was actually an incredibly glamorous coat. We almost regretted lending it to her – even mourned a little bit as we watched that coat flooshing out of the house, draped around our guest. It never came back.'

'What about your guest?' I asked. 'What became of her? Was she not contaminated somehow?'

'Hmm. No. I think she got a job in Wales.'

I realised that while the porter had been telling me her coat story, she had expertly gathered all of Big Andrew's bags and was leading me into the hotel lobby, which was vast and sleek. There were the squeaking noises of footsteps on polished concrete, echoing unseen from behind a distant partition.

Seeing the desk unattended, the porter sighed and put all of the bags down again. She went behind the desk. She quickly logged on to some system behind the desk, then whipped up her head as if she had been waiting there all along.

'Do you have a reservation?' she asked.

'No. Sorry. I, uh, I'm not really supposed to be here.'

'That's no problem. We have a room, but it's amongst the most basic in the hotel, I'm afraid. A simple en-suite. A three-quarter sized bed.'

'That's kind, thank you, but I really, I mean. I'm due to give a workshop later. I was just on my way to work, you know? I can't be too far from home, so I should be able to...' My voice trailed off as I realised it was impossible to explain my morning.

'Look, you don't have to stay the night if you don't want to. But, do you mind if I ask: if you were on your way to work, why do you have all these bags?'

'Oh.'

'They are your bags, aren't they? You haven't stolen them?'

'Ha ha! No. No-no-no, I haven't stolen them. More like a loan of them. I borrowed them.'

She blinked once and tilted her head to one side. 'I see. Do you want to take a look at our modest room? I can reserve it now, and then you can see what you think. There's no charge if it turns out you don't want to stay.'

I didn't want to make any commitments regarding the hotel room, so I backed away and took a breath. 'Listen,' I said. 'Do you think I could get a glass of juice or something? I could do with a sit down. Is there a – a bar or something? Or a lounge? I've had some bad news today. Terrible news, and I – to be perfectly honest, I haven't really had a chance to digest it.'

'Oh, I'm sorry to hear that. Sounds like you could use a drink? There is a bar and a lounge,' she pointed towards the distant partition where the squeaking sound still echoed occasionally.

The partition was more of a kind of chevron-shaped screen, pointing towards us. It was actually the separation point for two corridors.

'Choose left for the bar, or right for the lounge,' the porter said. 'Just along there.'

In the corridor to the left, there was half a photographic portrait visible. It seemed to be a portrait of Dr Dominic, the deputy head of my secondary school. Yes, an A1-sized Dr Dominic sitting in a leather chair, it seemed. A burgundy leather chair. It looked very natural, from where I was standing, for there to be such a portrait on this hotel wall.

It had been Dr Dominic who once found me and my friend sneaking out of school to go and buy sausage rolls. She told me she had made a discovery: the baker's across the road from the school would sell you a sausage roll *inside* a bread roll. With *butter!*

We were coming back in through the gates, eating these things, when Dr Dominic found us and asked what the hell was going on. He really screamed at us. He bared his teeth, I remember, and my friend smiled at him and said it was alright, and offered him some of her sausage roll within a bread roll. Only she could have done this, in all the world. Only she had enough charisma to offer that snack to that man in those circumstances.

'You can leave your bags with me. I'll have them taken to the room for you,' said the porter. 'There's no charge if you decide not to stay.'

'Ah, OK, that would actually be great, thank you.'

I walked towards the left-hand corridor. The photographic portrait turned out not to be of Dr Dominic after all, but a poster for an event: *M. A. GOOGAN. 3 P.M. SACKLER LOUNGE.*

M. A. Googan looked nothing like Dr Dominic after all. There were no details at all of what M. A. Googan would be doing at three o'clock, but it reminded me that that was the time I had been booked to give my workshop. I felt a little flutter of panic at the thought of them all there, eleven people, some of whom were fairly senior. If I ever tried to explain what happened to cause my absence, they would never understand.

My interest in the picture was cut short by the porter, who sort of gusted past me in her energetic way along the corridor.

'Hello again!' I said.

'See you in a sec,' she said, smiling. Although her smile was a little more strained than it had been earlier, a faint grimace as she headed, at speed, towards the bar area.

The corridor inched round in a long arc. As I followed the line of the wall, unable to see more than a metre or so ahead because of the curve, I became aware of a change in the atmosphere. The wall colour too had begun to change, from sterile white to a funky kind of taupish yellow. The polished concrete now had lush orange-and-rust carpet growing out of it, like sulphuric moss. The hard foot sounds of the lobby mellowed into a soft, easy chew. Soon, a kind of fibrous music reached my ears and I felt my walk go slack, freer, as I continued blindly down that tunnel, which was becoming like a kind of lovely ear canal.

It was no surprise to find the porter behind the polished black teak bar, shining a glass. She had a sort of laugh to herself about what she was doing while she poured my orange juice, which I had not yet ordered.

'Here,' she said. 'You look like there's a question on your mind.'

'Thanks. I guess I was wondering who M.A. Googan was.'

'Oh. Him! Don't talk to me about him.'

'Wow, really? Why not? I was only wondering because he looks a lot like my old deputy headmaster. But I don't think it was actually him.'

'No. I don't think so. He was meant to talk about skills gaps or something, but he cancelled. The audience is going to be furious.'

'The audience?'

'They're generalists. They come every week to see a different speaker. They get grumpy if we don't have a replacement when people cancel. Even when it's at the last minute.'

She stopped polishing the glass for a moment. 'Between us,' she said, 'this hotel relies on generalist audiences. Events, you know? They not only bring in immediate trade, but the audience all have friends. They've all got contacts and they recommend us. Conferences. Training weeks. Away days. Hotels like this – out of the way, in places with no tourism and no business – rely on that sort of thing, so looking after the generalists is hugely important.'

'When you say generalists...'

'They just come and listen to any speaker we put on. It barely matters what the topic is. Just general stuff. It can be anything. Sometimes just a memorial. Sometimes just a lecture. Just anything.'

'Like what?'

'You're really interested?'

'Yes.'

'Come with me.'

She solemnly put away the glass and the cloth and stepped out from behind the bar. She headed towards the stage area at the other end of the room. It was a low stage, rigged more for music than for business – a mike stand, amplifiers, space for a drum kit, all dressed in gold and brown staging panels, like a variety television show.

'This way,' she said. She sounded excited. She was half-skipping as we crossed the stage and turned left into a small backstage area, where she opened up a low cupboard in the wall.

'This way,' she said.

I followed her through the low cupboard into a negative version of the bar we had just been in. It was like a cathedral, but also like a horror loft.

'This is the neutral space of the hotel,' she said. 'One of our very first speakers came to talk about the difference between a neutral and a negative space.'

'But surely this is just a room?'

'Technically not. This is like a crawl space, you know? But bigger. There's no access except through that little cupboard. It can't legally be treated as a room. It's got to exist, but only in a neutral sense. Walk around,' she said.

As I shuffled around in the dark, the porter told me that the architect who designed the hotel was famed for accidentally ending up with these monstrous caverns of negative space. No matter how hard she tried, the architect would always end up needing to include walls that faced into one another, creating secret, pointless uses of the building's footprint.

'The speaker who came to talk about it came all the way from Sydney. She begged us for access to the neutral space. It was beautiful, we brought in candles and she cried five or six times while she talked about how the architect had eventually gone insane when the negative space of a business park she designed in Madrid was actually spatially more substantial than the surrounding, usable building. She gave up in the end, and now works as a sound engineer in a small semi-professional theatre company.'

I continued to explore the neutral space. There was just enough half-light to see there was nothing on the ground. It was smooth, only slightly grainy underfoot. The walls that loomed above were a mess, cluttered and flapping with loose insulation wadding, the dark foamy corners lurking like a flock.

'It goes up a way,' I said. The ceiling was not visible, save for a few specks of light, far above us.

I noticed that the porter was standing next to me. She was sort of febrile. She reminded me of my friend who had died, who had never stood still, and who was always about to laugh. I had a strong physical memory of being in the presence of her strange athleticism. A strength that felt at once focused yet utterly unpredictable.

I was weeping pretty openly.

'I remember her so vividly. She was there at school, bobbing next to me with this exaggerated goofball walk, and a smile that encompassed her entire head. She was an athlete and a clown. She was a comic genius.'

'That's a nice memory.'

'Yeah. With the sun on our backs, walking from the classroom to the field, and the blue sky, laughing at something plainly unfunny. It's nothing. It's all I have of her. I wish she was here.'

I wept more. It was pretty ugly really, but in the dark it didn't seem to matter.

'I'm sorry,' I said. 'I've had the weirdest day.'

'Don't worry,' said the porter. 'Some things happen that just don't make any sense. But afterwards, everything carries on.'

We stood in the dark for a few seconds. I told the porter that I had a workshop prepared, if her generalists could cope with hearing about API documentation.

She said that sounded fine.

'Do you think we could do it in here? In the dark?'

'Yeah, sure,' said the porter. 'They're always happy to sign the insurance waiver and come back here.'

Before I ran my workshop, I put on some of Big Andrew's clothes. One of his shirts and a pair of incredibly soft trousers. They felt all silky and wonderful against my body.

It was a good session. One of my best, conducted with the generalist audience politely standing in a row, in the dark, each sensing the movement of the person next to them, like friends are known to do, at the funerals of their friends.

LIFELONG LEARNING

'Tell us, why have you come here?' That's what they will ask. The village leaders will look at you in a serious way and say, 'Please, in your own time, tell us why you are here.'

'Cheapest place,' you will say with a minor shrug. 'Not easy to get to, which also suits me.'

And then you will casually cough. Or perform some other mysterious action. You might spit, instead of coughing. Or both? No. One or the other. You can't both cough and spit because that would look like a medical thing and they don't want medical problems there, according to your very limited reading about the village, which you had to do in the half-light at the back of the cupboard in Jill's kitchen.

After you have coughed or spat or whatever you decide is the best move, the village leaders will smile professionally, and give you time to elaborate on your reasons. 'We are looking for the true reasons,' they will say. They will give you time in which to gather yourself.

'I have been,' you will begin. 'I have been feeling somewhat a...'

You won't see much mileage in this approach, so you will start again.

'There have been...'

You will stop.

'I have been,' you will begin again. 'I – that is to say –'

You will not finish this either. You will try:

'I'm sorry, I can't.'

'I don't know how to explain.'

'There was a...'

You can't imagine finishing many sentences, but you feel as though they will get used to that, in the village. They will say, 'That's alright, isn't it?'

One of the kindlier leaders will pat you on the arm. Just there, on the top of the arm, 'That's alright, isn't it? We don't need to know it all at once. We get the picture.'

That's what you hope. That they will get the picture.

You are walking along a path through a strong mist. Your clothes are damp, especially at the neck of your jumper. This is real, you think. There are beads of mist caught in your hair. This is really actually happening. You are going to a place called the village. You do not feel adequately able to describe why, but it is a wonderful feeling. Like being in a cloud – a sensation you have always wanted to feel.

The mist is so thick, that when you do see people, they appear as lit heads, or figurines, at the verge of the path you seem to be following without being able to fully see. They variously tell you to turn back, or to keep going. You feel as though they are trying to trick you.

'This journey is not for the faint hearted,' a boy said to you a while back. A boy of ten or eleven, saying it as though he was reciting a line he had to say in a school assembly. He was with his mother and father at the side of the path, all of them passing food to each other. Drinks and sandwiches, wholesome pieces of fruit and white bread.

'Leave the travellers alone,' the father said. 'Have a berry.'

'But that one has left someone behind!' the boy insisted.

'If they have, it was for the best,' said the mother who had the light of the sun on her face despite the fog around her. And somewhere there was the sound of the boy's sister, humming a lovely tune.

Everything that is happening to you is real.

You want to go back and say something to the family, something about how they made you feel with their comments and their food, but you cannot go back. You want to go back and look at the sun on the face of the mother, how she was alive with sunlight, but you have missed it. It is the same feeling as when you find yourself missing the bit of your favourite song. The moment you have been living for, that sweet height the music brings you to when you give it your full attention, but it is gone now, and rewinding won't work.

It was the best idea, definitely, to leave Carl at the party. Carl cannot come to the village with you. Certainly not. Even the short distance you have come on this long journey has confirmed, once and for all, that you have outgrown your association with Carl. You are no longer the person who met Carl, at the agreed service station, at seven a.m., on the agreed working days.

You are no longer the person who got into Carl's silver car, and sat in his passenger seat and listened to his music and breathed in his B&H smoke (then later, vanilla and cherry vape) as he drove you to the assessments offices of the insurance company where you were both working. You are no longer that person who allowed Carl, a man eleven years older than you and yet seemingly no further along with things, to run your life.

'There's a hole in your ear!' Carl once said. You were in his spare room, during a phase in which you weren't going out because Carl wanted things to be home-based. He wanted to save money. He was sick of going out. He was doing two or three major washes a day, and there were damp clothes everywhere.

You did not know what was going in until you were hit by the cold and the stink of the lager. You could suddenly feel the foam swelling inside your head. Yes, Carl had poured Grolsch into your ear, while you were asleep. There was some on the pillow.

'Fucking hell!' He announced. 'Fucking hell – where did it go? It's gone directly into your head! All of it! Christ! You ear is a portal! A fucking hole!'

Carl was a great believer in the concept of the holes. He used to say they were everywhere. Some of them were absolutely miniscule – tinier than a neutron – but they were all capable of expanding. They weren't black holes, he would say, correcting you. Just these holes that you could fall into. Anything could fall into them, depending on the size of the hole. He was fascinated by where the holes lead to. Probably nowhere, was his most common conclusion.

He apologised somewhat, about the beer he had poured into your ear. He could see how upset it had made you. He gave you one of the pillows from his bed and all the rest of it, but he wasn't really sorry. He was more interested, much more interested in the fact that none of the beer he had poured in had come out of your ear.

'I poured in over half the can!' he said. 'There was no overflow. Nothing. You have to accept that it's weird. Like, you tipped your head, didn't you?'

You told him that you had tipped your head, yes.

'And nothing came out.'

'No, nothing came out.'

'You've got to admit,' he said. 'You've got to admit that's worth further investigation.' He came at you, approaching the ear with his finger that he had wettened by sucking.

This should have been the day that you finally moved on from Carl, the day of the wet finger ear, but it wasn't. There were many more days after.

But it did make you wonder, about the holes. And it did make you sometimes put your finger, just a bit too far, into your right ear.

Before you moved into Carl's spare room, things had been silent. There were those whole weeks in which you saw nobody outside of the corner shop and the stairs to your flat. Slowly, you felt your friends move away – your real friends – and there was nothing going on anymore, except the things Carl invited you to.

He took you to the places that you had normally swerved to avoid. He took you into pubs with reflective surfaces. He gave you different premium vodkas and told you about the distillation process while he watched you drinking them.

He was relentless with your time – you could never quite get home without him demanding a drink, or hauling you to some non-specific work event. There were birthdays of people you worked with but had never met – people from a completely different part of the company. There were anniversary drinks, leaving drinks, or just drink drinks, or fuck-it-I've-had-enough drinks.

If you tried to slip away early, he'd somehow be there, lurking near the door with a cigarette for you, and a shot of something that tasted of sugar in mouthwash. 'Come and meet Del,' he would say. Or, 'Sam's gonna be here in a minute, and Muppet. You don't want to miss that, that's the whole reason we came out!' Or, 'Don't leave me with them, please. I'm begging you! Not with these fucking numbskulls. Just stay for one more! I'm buying, you tight fucker!'

And you would accept it – the drink, the offer of meeting Muppet or Del. When the night was over, he would get a cab, but never offer to drop you home. It was always, 'Crash at mine,' with Carl. In time, the sofa became a place you slept regularly. He had a blanket, and he called it *your blanket*. 'I'll just get your blanket then,' he would say.

You stopped expecting to go home after work. In addition to *your blanket*, you now had *your little bag of shit* round at Carl's, which contained a bundle of socks, underwear, a spare toothbrush. Gradually, you added more of your clothes to this bag until it contained a full weekly rotation. At first, Carl would put your clothes in the wash with his own. He even folded them in a pile and made a joke about being your new mum. This didn't last, of course. Long after he stopped adding your clothes into his own cycle – insisting instead that you take your bag to the laundrette, along with a few of his own choice garments to make up the wash – he was still telling people at work that he did your washing, and that you had once called him Mum by mistake.

It was October, you remember Halloween shit in all the shops, when after three nights at Carl's, you snuck home one afternoon to try and sleep off the tail end of a Jäger-hangover and discovered that the electricity had gone – the emergency money on the meter had burned out and the freezer was leaking in the kitchen. Your money situation was so dire, you didn't bother to get the card refilled. You slept in the cold for two days straight, texting Carl to ask him to cover for you at work.

He came to your place on the third day. He sat you at the kitchen table. 'Look around you,' he said. 'This is not life.' He showed you the bills, he held them in front of your face. 'You're fucked, pal,' he said. He told you it was a write off. He showed you the final total amount you owed. 'You're never going to pay this off on your own.'

While you stared at the pile and shrugged, he quietly gathered the precious pictures from the fridge and put them in a plastic bag. Then without realising it, you fell into Carl's cycle completely: you took the spare room at his house, to save money, because you had absolutely no money at all.

Your life became a vision of legs appearing in the crack of the doorway, as you were awoken by the sound of people you did not know walking through the corridor, burping and plodding in the living room. You never saw faces, just these thick hairy frightening legs. All his friends – all of them – churning through day-on-day, their belongings slowly building up around you. Left behind hats. Lent, but unwanted, DVDs. These people were in your life constantly, for all the long months of you and Carl.

Turning to look back, you are not surprised to find that all traces of the little door have vanished from sight. If you wanted to get back into the party, even if you wanted to do that, you couldn't anymore. You are heading away, to the village, where they will ask you why you have come, and you will try your hardest to finish a sentence. You sense that you are very close to the point of no return. Or maybe, you have reached the point where reaching the point of no return has itself become inevitable.

You can hear the sound of bells above an old shop door. You cannot see the door, but it must be there, somewhere in the fog.

'Hello?' you say.

'Just keep going,' says a voice in the darkness. You see the shape of someone passing by, the outline of a country person – maybe a maid? – in an old costume, and her skin is weather beaten.

'If you know what's good for you, you won't stop moving,' says the voice, and then the person, or the shape of a person, is gone.

The ground under your feet has changed. The cupboardy, damp chipboard sponge has given way to a stone feeling. It is uneven but there's no suggestion you will trip. You are far away. You have really left the party, and you have really left Carl and life with Carl, all behind.

Poor Carl. In a way, yes. Poor Carl. It had been negative for him too, your time in each other's lives. He had been stagnating. He must have noticed how little you thought of him.

Recently he had taken to coming into the spare room where you sleep, immediately after he'd been having sex with someone in his own bedroom. He'd come in and sit on your bed, smelling bleakly of condom lubricant.

The first few times, he would come in and tell you about the sex he'd had. You'd lie there, trying to work out a way to make him go away, with your eyes firmly shut, and wondering who the person in his room was, and how she was feeling. You could not simply scream at Carl to get out because you owed him (you still owe him) so much money.

You barely had enough money to speak. You barely had enough money to even move. When you had an income, everything would be sent directly to your creditors, and any leftover pennies would be gone within a few days. On wine. On cigarettes that Carl smoked in the house, in your room, on your bed, naked in his pale kimono.

'This is depressing for us, it really is,' he would say sometimes. 'Just so demoralising.'

And on it would go, the rest of the month with absolutely nothing in the bank and nothing going on. Carl, curry sauce, television, the cold leather sofa with an actual mouse potentially living inside it. 'I can hear it!' Carl would declare, and he would leap up and start hitting the sofa with his fist. He would be laughing, but he would be hitting the sofa so hard the sound of it made your ears buzz.

And then one morning – this morning – after you had just read the text from work telling you that you weren't needed (and would not be needed again because the whole company was going to the wall) you found him on the sofa with that smile on his face. The one he was convinced was dangerous and roguish and intelligent, but actually made him look drunk and unappealing.

'Carl, have you seen what's happening? What are we going to do?'

'Fuck it. We'll get severance.'

'Will we?'

'Yes. Stop worrying.' He waved a hand through the air. The money that had been coming into your account, that little pulse of currency that swelled and then immediately emptied as the direct debits kicked in, had been all you were clinging onto. Now there was nothing except Carl and his fucking smile.

'Party tonight, isn't it?' He said. 'Piss up for Roland. You know he's leaving?'

'Oh yeah. Roland.'

'Yeah, he's leaving for Abu Dhabi.'

'Right. Yeah. At Jill's is it?'

'Yeah.'

There was then the silence during which you felt trapped because you were going to have to ask to be excused the rent again this month. You had nothing. You had nothing whatsoever, and the nothingness was an actual chemical, churning your stomach. While Carl looked at you with that smile on his face, telling you about how Abu Dhabi was the place to be. Get rich. Pay no tax. Nobody gave a shit what you did there if you were English.

It took all of your strength to reply. Just to get some words out. And the words you said were not adequate for Carl to shut up, so he went on, telling you about his cousin who once flew a helicopter for rich pricks in Dubai. 'Gack everywhere with those people,' he said. 'Didn't matter that you could get beheaded. Gack and Bollinger and cash and fucking. The free life,' he said. He loved to refer to the free life.

He took your card to the corner shop, used your emergency overdraft allowance on organic cider, which you drank warm.

Then, before you knew it, it was time for the fucking party.

'Don't worry about it, Jill,' Carl said when you arrived at the party. 'It's got the strop on today.'

Then to the rest of the room, still calling you 'it', he said, 'Don't pay any attention to it everybody, you'll just make it worse. It's got the full arsehole!'

That was Carl's way of announcing that you had lost your job, and now you had to find a new job, but you were here at the party all the same and willing to have a good time.

You entered the living room and sat down on the sofa. You lit a cigarette, and then Jill came in with a drink for you. It was a blue-coloured WKD. She said that she was sorry about the job and not to worry because you are clever and will easily find work, and then she slumped sideways onto you on the sofa and made a sympathetic groaning noise. Some others were gathered round on the hard dining table chairs, drinking and not making eye contact. 'Don't worry mate,' one of them said. 'It'll be fine,' said another one. 'Fuck it,' said a third.

You drank your drink and smoked another cigarette and you heard about Jill's plan to buy new shelves.

In the background there was the constant sound of 'Call of Duty', and the smell of smokers coming in from outside, bitter with hash.

When your drink was finished, you went to the kitchen. You put the empty bottle on the counter and looked for another blue WKD.

There was a cupboard hanging open next to the bin. The hinge was broken, so the door dangled clumsily. It was obvious that there was no WKD in the cupboard, but you opened it anyway.

It was full of crockery and baking trays with skins of old grease and fibres of dust. It was obvious that you should not climb into this cupboard, but you climbed into it anyway.

You pushed your way to the back of the cupboard, which was enormous and filled with a strange mist.

You sat down in the dark, your hand touched the cold corner of something. A short book. You angled the book towards the light. It was called *Opportunities for Lifelong Learning at the Village*. You sat in the phenomenally cave-like back of the cupboard and read all about the reasons and ways people were welcomed to the village.

In the grey light, another figure approaches, a shrouded figure, lurching, singing in a whisper.

'Oh,' it says, 'I remember. Do you remember John?'

You look at the figure, and you see glamorous sequined things under its rags, shining out, strips of red and gold tight against a firm body. The smell is very disco, or so it seems, but the rags on the outside are what matters to the figure. Its voice does not belong to disco, or the strong alcoholic flavour of the figure's perfume. You look into the rags and you see, through them, the stain of a face. As you stare into the blotch of one of the figure's eyes, you realise that you do remember John. You remember him singing to you. You remember him lifting you up in the air.

'Yes,' you say, 'I remember John.'

'You remember John!'

'I remember John.'

'The singing?'

'I remember John singing a song about the gallows to me. I came in while he was on the toilet, and I turned to go, but he said, it's alright, come in. So I sat on my step, the step I used to stand on so I could reach the toilet. I asked John what the song was called – but I didn't really call him John...'

'He was in a tight white vest.'

'He was in a tight white vest, he was. Yes. I asked him to sing me the song. So he sang a song about being clamped in irons. Then he sang 'Forever Blowing Bubbles'. But I never called him John. What do you want to know about him?' you asked the figure.

'Just if you remember John.'

'I don't think it can be the same man. I remember another John,' you say. 'A different one.'

You desperately want to talk about the other John, who in fact was a Jon, and was very dear to you. A dear and treasured Jon. You try to turn back to discuss the subject of this other Jon, but it is not possible.

'Just keep going,' says the figure.

You try to persuade the figure to talk more to you, but there's no way of doing this. You will never get to talk about the other Jon. A friend, a true friend.

You will also never know why this figure has chosen to disguise its obvious love of funky music with these stained rags.

You walk on. Two Johns. One in a vest. One in a shirt most of the time, or a soft cotton T-shirt. Very soft.

The John you remembered first, it's true, was always wearing that tight white vest, but even so, as he sang his songs, you could see sideways the sad effect gravity had on his chest fat. Two fleshy duck necks, nubbing at his tight white vest.

The road has broadened, and you are on the outskirts of a conurbation. It's dusk. Purple sky, rolling hills and the sparse jabs of light where there are buildings with windows. It could be the village.

'I've travelled a long way,' you will say. 'Can I simply, for this one night at least, can I rest? And tomorrow, if that's alright, we can discuss the reasons I've come. We can discuss my qualifications and so on tomorrow.'

But first, there is this question of the distance because, in fact, the hills are fairly severe. Even though you can see the lights, there is a long way to travel yet.

You read about the village shop and the café. You read about the long-term lodgings, and the possibilities for work, and the relatively low cost of living. You read about the sympathetic way the village leaders were sure to look at someone like you – someone who could not identify why they felt nothing at all – and you decided to fully push through and leave for good. You had read literature about cupboards as a child – the possibilities of leaving through them – and you had witnessed the ability to absorb an entire can of premium lager into a cavity in your ear, so this seemed fine.

And it is real. This is real.

Based on the reading you did in the cupboard, the secretive admission policy casts a long shadow over the village. You have to be qualified to live there.

'Are you?' they will say. 'Are you qualified?' You read the criteria, but it was so vague in some places, and so point-lessly specific in others.

Are you feeling somewhat withdrawn?

When did you last make yourself fully understood in a work or a private context?

Is there something you can do to help fellow villagers, for example can you make egg substitutes from flax seed at scale?

You did not bring the guide with you. The single clear-est instruction was that you cannot travel with the guide, it must be read and then left where you found it, for the next person who wants to come.

'I'm vulnerable,' you will be able to tell them in all honesty. 'I've had lots of problems.'

'Have you run away before?' they might ask.

'Many times, but never far. A lot of attempts, yes, of different kinds. But this is different.'

And they will nod, maybe. You hope they will nod. From looking at the guide, which had only a sort of line drawing of the questioning procedure, it seems like they either nod or they don't nod.

The reading material promised that you would not be sent away. Newcomers, it implied, are very welcome to talk to the owner of the shop or the proprietor of the café about renting a room for a few days, during the questioning process, before securing more long-term accommodation.

Yes, it's a good thing that you took advantage while you had the chance, of that kitchen cupboard door being very slightly open at Jill's house. They will be looking for you now, but that's ok. They can keep looking. They won't think of looking in the cupboard for a tunnel that leads away from the house and towards the village.

Almost definitely, this was a one-time hole. None of Jill's other guests will be able to get through the cupboard. You have left. You have left all of it behind.

Another voice in the dark, this time agitated, reading out loud from a newspaper. It's hard to understand what is being read. The voice seems to be coming from a low down place, like it is being spoken by someone stooping, or, as you realise when you see the person speaking, someone struggling to see the words.

You slow your walk, soften your steps, try not to breathe. The owner of the voice seems to find a steady angle to read an obituary of the owners of a house that recently got sucked away. The family who died in the sucking away of the house are not mentioned. The obituary seems to be more of the house itself. It was once a celebrated work of romantic architecture. It was the building, the figure tries to make you understand, that had been the real tragedy.

The great house had been conceived in a fit of passion by a fevered Earl. The great staircase, the centrepiece and spine of the building, was made of marble fused together around strands of ligaments taken from the musculature of the earl's favourite horse.

'Would you remember that house,' the voice asks you. 'if you went back again?'

'No, I don't think I would,' you reply. 'I don't think I've ever been to such a place.'

'Oh yes,' the voice said. 'You went there twice. Once on a school trip. You went to admire the statues in the lawns and do brass rubbings on the graves. And there was a second time, the time you went with your grandmother, and you ruined her day.'

As you hear the word 'grandmother', the mist through which you have been struggling liquifies in your mouth, thickening into oil, almost choking you.

'Yes, do you recall?' the voice says. Now the speaker, a stooped wretch, is circling you, spitting words at you.

'You would not stop asking for something in the gift shop and your patient, sweet grandmother went grey in the skin around her mouth. She gathered her bag and left you in the gift shop. You watched her barge another elderly woman out of the way.

'So selfish, but it is gone now,' says the voice. 'Your appalled grandmother. Your incessant asking. It is gone, now. All sucked away, along with that amazing house.'

The stooped figure finishes their little attack on your memories with a flourish, but you press ahead. The figure was right. There were two visits to that famous house: one time with Grandmother, who was, yes, greatly ashamed. She was indeed grey in the skin and upset, but she forgave you. You feel certain she forgave you.

The visit you remember most was the visit with the school.

You were with Jon – your old friend Jon – and your other friends Kevin and Bryn and Rachel and Kate (all the Kates) and Laura (all the Lauras) and Jack and Naomi but you got separated from them. You were all looking at the statue of the horse, and when you looked back, you were separated. You were alone.

The museum security guard watched you, there to stop any harm coming to the statue of the horse. He watched you try to work out which way to go: into the vast grounds, where it was hot and meltingly bright, where light dazzled off the lake and pollen sweated on every slow breath of air; or into the house, that weird dark house where you had seen several paintings of nothing but a black space, and in the recesses of the dark paint, certain disturbed faces that seemed to have been dragged there, into existence, as if cursed.

'You seem to find yourself in a predicament,' the guard said to you eventually. He had a nasty sort of smile on his face. 'They have all left you behind,' he said. 'You have become friendless.'

And you stood alone next to the cool white horse, under the gaze of the museum security guard. You stood alone for the entirety of the lunch hour, completely without friends.

You press on through the stubborn mist. You are starting to know what you will say.

'Why have you come here?' they will ask.

'I hope to find someone,' you will say. 'Because I have been alone on the limits for so long. I have been in need of my friends for so long.'

You keep going, towards the punched-out lights, and you hope that you know you will qualify.

RACHEL REACHES OUT

Rachel reached out to Theo, and then she waited.

Theo was supposed to have come back to her days ago, but he had not come back to her. She was now virtually begging.

Me again!

Hi Theo,

Are we still doing the retrograde testing? Only I have to complete this high-level for Paul L and Retrograde is the only thing still outstanding, I'm afraid.

Sorry to be a bore. Also, Retrograde – Is that even the right word!?!? I can never remember!

Come back to me quick, yeah. :p

Rach

She hit send and sighed as the email-whoosh came through her headphones. Theo was sitting at his desk less than six metres away, but she couldn't just go over because he was on a call. Theo was always on a call. He'd been given a lot more responsibility since the shake-up in May, and now everyone in the whole of SME/APU wanted a piece of his ass. She would just have to wait.

There was a ping from Paul L:

Rach, just following up, are you able to send over the actions for QR team?

> Hi Paul!
> Sure, np. Just sending now.
> Was waiting for Theo to come back to me
> about some test lag but I can actually complete
> the actions without his input, if that's OK?

Sure. Do you want me to lean on Theo?

> No no – it's fine. Can finish actions,
> then add Theo to chain.

Great ☺ Lucky theo ;)

> Lol – I know. We need like ten of him! ;)

Lol.

She finished the actions document. It was only three actions, but it had taken her more than a week. She wondered if Paul L noticed that he had to chase her for every tiny thing these days. He probably did. Of course he did. So why didn't he mention it?

She wondered if he was bottling it up. Then she wondered if he slagged her off to his wife.

His wife was very Christian, apparently, but she would need an outlet. Rachel imagined her name being cursed in the Paul L family kitchen. Over the butter? But she couldn't see it. Maybe they didn't slag anyone off at Paul L's home. Paul L was probably really not like that.

Whoosh. Actions, gone.

Next, she had a clear hour before anyone was going to trouble her for anything, so Rachel got out her Paperchase notebook and a 0.7mm mechanical pencil. She drew a quick sketch of an idea for a clothing brand she had come up with. It was basically just blankets. Or sleeping bags. But shaped so they could be worn as clothes. The brand name was going to be SLUGS. People had all sorts of stupid names for things, was her reasoning. She could imagine really raw, no-make-up people wearing their SLUGS clothes outside in the city at sunset. They would be in this kind of hazy, post-apocalypse-y light, and the models would look at the camera in a way that implied maybe they were dead or a new genus or something – a shade of human that did not need to rush around in an emergency, anyway.

She wrote SLUGS in a number of different ways. Then she carefully outlined a male model with zero body fat, swathed in a SLUGS blanket. She spent twenty minutes shading him. She felt quietly guilty for wasting so much time, but Theo was still on his call. Nobody gave a single fuck about her, or anything she did, was the truth.

After another ten minutes, she gave up on the drawing, which had become unwieldy and over-detailed. By the time she slung down her pencil, the male model's lips and eyes were inhuman, or like a bad skin graft.

She put away her Paperchase notebook and scanned through the rest of her emails. She touched in with a few people regarding meeting rooms that were confirmed as booked for some meetings she was down to chair. Only one thing of interest came into her inbox.

Firmwide Announcement

Dear colleagues,

I am delighted to announce that after thirty years with the firm, Jocylin Haggus has been promoted to head of IT SEC and TET in our New York office. Jocylin will be replacing Dan Shanks, who is leaving us after ten years in senior management.

We want you to join us in wishing both of them well in their new roles, both inside and outside of the firm.

With warm wishes,

Glen Crooke

CEO

Rachel took a little breath.

RE: Firmwide Announcement

Dear Jocylin,

Congratulations! I'm sure you don't remember me, but we met a few years ago when I was out doing training in Shanghai. I think it might even have been seven years! Gosh, how time has flown.

Anyway – I remember you gave me some really good advice

when we met, and I think it's just wonderful that you are being given a broader leadership role in the firm.

You're an inspiration.

With fondest regards,

Rachel Payant

London SEC

At the whoosh, Rachel made the sound of pretending to be sick.

Time slipped. She sat and just stared at the top of her screen for a bit. Then, since it was already eleven o'clock, she decided to go and get ready for her gym session, which was at twelve thirty. She was determined to go to Zappa Spin today. She was determined, for once, to attend the session she had paid for. It did not matter who else was going.

It did not.

She pressed refresh on her emails one more time. After a few moments of silence while nobody emailed her, she grabbed her rucksack and headed to the toilets.

In the toilets, she looked at her skin in the mirror. She had been drawing her skin recently, during meetings. A kind of landscape of herself, the cross sections of skin that you get in textbooks. She liked that the layers of the Earth's crust looked basically the same as layers of skin, until you added labels and detail. When it was just lines, human skin could be anything.

Rachel didn't know the names of the layers of skin, so her labels said things like, 'hair', but there were multiple hair-type things to label, so she added also 'fronds'. Fronds, hairs, hilly area, porous zone, lymphs. She drew squiggles here and there with great, seething motion to represent bacteria.

While looking in the mirror, she pulled at her cheek.

She rolled her fingers around on her temples. She was breathing, she was breathing fine. 'At Zappa Spin, your breathing will be so even,' she told herself. 'This time, you are going to do exactly what Xavier tells you to do. You are going to Zapp-app-app-app to the fucking absolute limit.'

'Hi Rachel,' said Jane. Jane was from the QR team. Jane was crushing the ends of her hair in her fist whilst looking at her reflection.

'Hi Jane,' Rachel said.

'Rachel! Look at my hair. Are you coming to spin today?'

There was a short pause before Rachel said, 'No.' She clenched her jaw very, very hard until her teeth hurt.

'Oh,' said Jane. 'That's a shame. I thought you were definitely, definitely coming this time.'

'Yeah, I know. I definitely, definitely was. But. I know it's stupid. Stupid stupid, but I just don't feel like I can do it today. I'm just going to do my normal circuit.'

'Oh that's a shame,' said Jane again. 'I was hoping. Because then I'd have someone. I find it so intimidating!'

'Ha. Sorry. I know what you mean, but I – I can't. I need to take it easy, I think. I think I have a slight chest infection coming on. There was an atmospheric event, in one of the other buildings where I live. Quite a bad one actually, and a lot of trouble got into my maisonette. So.'

'Oh gosh!'

'Yeah, so.'

'So, and that's given you a chest infection? Shouldn't you be resting? Rachel, I'm worried about you.'

Jane was now looking at Rachel with a kind of contempt. The culture was, if you're sick or infectious in any way then you stay at home and recover quickly.

'No, no. Jane, seriously. I mean, the doctor said there's

nothing at all to worry about. No reason to keep away from work.'

'No, but.'

'But, you know, my hair seems to have the smell in it.'

'Oh God. OK, yeah.'

'The smell of... whatever it was? And I just feel like.... I'm fine, but... You know. I'll just do my plod on the treadmill and then a few sit ups and then just squats maybe and crunches. Sorry!'

'No, don't be!'

'I'm going on!'

'No, Rachel. I mean something like that, even nearby. It's... I understand.'

'It's nothing, really.'

'I mean, it sounds very non-specific, but it sounds dreadful.'

Rachel said a few more things to Jane and then left the toilet. She had a quick stare at her motionless inbox. Nobody was around. Theo wasn't at his desk. Nor was Paul L.

At the gym, Rachel crushed out 6K on the running machine, incline at 3.0 and speed 9. She watched her face degrade in the mirror as her vision greyed and blotched. She could smell burnt wood in her sweat.

She was still vaguely panting and aware of the faint smell of smoke when she got back to her desk and refreshed her emails again. There was something from Paul L.

Serious Matter

Rach,

Need to talk urgently if poss. Theo wants to clear a few things up, if that's cool. We are in 701 Green.

Regards

P L

RE: Serious Matter

Sure – of course, Paul. I'll be right there.

Best

Rach

Paul L was sitting in the central seat at the long board-room table in 701. Theo was on Paul's right, looking at the wall. Rachel took a chair opposite them both. It was the same set up as when they had done a team huddle in here, and everyone had laughed at Theo's withering critique of the enormousness of the table.

Paul L was one of those men who cycled everywhere. He went to church and he had two kids in a good school near his village. You imagined that Paul L could probably kill someone with his bare hands, because of all the exercise he did. And because of the veins in his wrists, and the moon-crater radii of his temples.

Theo was just Theo. He wore a shitty shirt that was either once white and was now grey, or had always been grey but was such an ugly grey that nobody normal would buy it. He wore black jeans even though it was meant to be business casual firmwide. Theo had a patchy black beard and black spectacles. He had zero sex appeal, and yet Rachel found him sexy. Sexy Theo, that's what she called him.

On the table between Paul and Theo was a printed email.

'Rach!' said Paul, smiling broadly. 'I am avoiding saying anything official because this isn't yet official, but if you want us to go down any official channels, then, you know, just say so and we will stop and get in the appropriate people et cetera swiftly and move things in that direction.'

'OK. I don't really,' said Rachel. 'I mean, this is fine. I.'

'So, Theo showed me the email you sent him, and he feels that it might not have been appropriate for the office. He's agreed that we should check with you first, before taking anything to the next level? Just to see if this was a mistake or an, erm, I guess typo would be stretching it...'

Theo didn't look at Rachel, he was staring at the wall opposite him, so all Rachel saw was his profile. It was hard to tell for sure, but he looked like he was shaking. Physically shaking.

'Well,' said Rachel, 'I don't know which email. So I...'

'You called me a retard!' blurted Theo, still staring at the wall. 'You called me a flipping *retard*!'

He sounded so wounded, Rachel thought he might cry. She felt a sudden and all-consuming surge of rage towards Theo and his emotions.

'I – What? What? Paul. I didn't call him a – I would never – I would just never use that word.'

'Mmm. Yeah. But, here is the email,' said Paul. He pushed the printed email along the table to her.

Tardigrade

Hi Theo,

I am a tardigrade.

Love from,

Rach

Paul watched her reading over his steepled hands. 'It says you sent it this morning, just before we spoke.'

Rachel read the email again. 'I didn't send this.'

Paul nodded, 'I checked with the server guys and it definitely came from your machine, when you were sitting there, so.'

'But I didn't write this. Or. I mean, even if I did, Theo. This doesn't say "you're a retard". Does it? It says, "I am a tardigrade". So I mean...'

'Yes,' said Paul. 'That was my feeling too. Theo, do you think you could see it like that? That Rach actually was calling herself a tardigrade, and not calling you a retard?'

Theo didn't move. He just stared straight at the wall.

'What is a tardigrade, anyway?' said Paul.

'I don't know,' said Rachel. 'I really didn't intend at all to write this word. I did send Theo an email but it was much longer and –'

'I might just look it up,' said Paul.

Nobody said anything else for an entire minute. Paul L had to dismiss a couple of messages on his phone before he could do the search. Eventually, he looked up at Rachel. 'Oh, it's like a kind of insect or something. Or, no. It's a water bear. Wow – look at that thing!'

Paul L held up his phone so that Rachel too could be fascinated by the close-up image of a tardigrade. It looked like a giant vampire maggot. It had about a million teeth. It looked like an alien.

Rachel tried to marshal her thoughts. She cleared her throat and sat up as straight as she could while she spoke. 'Anyway, I don't know how my email ended up saying anything about tardigrades. I am sorry, Theo. I was actually writing about the retrograde testing. Which you are very late getting back to me about. Maybe, somehow, tardigrade is similar? I don't know. Anyway. I would never use that word, retard, and I didn't call you anything, so... so... actually, could you please look at me?'

Theo didn't look up.

'Theo, please look at me!'

'Theo's pretty busy at the moment, actually Rach,' said Paul, interlocking his long fingers. 'In fact, I think he's probably on a call now.'

Rachel noticed for the first time that Theo was wearing tiny headphones. He was nodding absently, as though listening to another conversation. After a few more seconds, Paul stood up and ushered Rachel back to her desk. Then he pinged to send her home for the day.

At home, Rachel watched a television drama in which hundreds of people were crammed into a hospital corridor in various states of incineration. There had been some kind of major event in Bristol, was the premise. There was a constant sound of sirens, and the voices of doctors and nurses screaming urgent information to each other.

Rachel found it hard to look at the TV light, her eyes were sort of aching. Possibly because of the negativity that had found its way into her maisonette, and possibly because she had slept with her contact lenses in three times this year.

Whatever it was, looking at the light gave her a headache, so instead, she stared at the space just above her television. She imagined that she was in a dream and in fact everything she was watching, and everything she had ever watched on television, or read in a book, or seen in a gallery or at the cinema, all of it was something she had created herself, inside her dream. And she was, right now, just asleep in a room, a sweet, comfortable room, many years in what she thought of as 'the past'.

Every fashion statement and every song and work of architecture were all in the palace of her imagination. Soon, she imagined, she would wake in an asylum in some soft and boring reality and she would be able to create the world's greatest work from scratch.

Her mobile phone rang. It was Ben P.

'Rach! What the fuck is going on? Why haven't you called me back?'

'Hi Ben.'

'Seriously! You silly slag, what are you like? Why haven't you called me back? I'm worried about you. Rachel? Can you hear me? Rachel?'

'Jesus, Ben, shut up. I'm not in the mood.'

'Rachel do you remember the atmospheric event? You've had everyone so worried, Rachel.'

'I said I'm fine. It was in another block. I'm fine.'

'Rachel? You're breaking up.'

Ben P was gone, but a text arrived a few minutes later.

Sorry, bad signal. Just worried about you, but you seem fine, you massive Tardigrade!!!!!! ;)

Rachel screamed a bit, and tried to call Ben P. back, but it was just his voicemail. He had one of those voicemail messages that is just heavy breathing. Ben P. was in fact disgusting. At university, where they met, he was always asking her about her sex life. As her housemate, Ben P.'s first ever present to her was a kind of comedy vibrator. The whole memory of him made her turn off the television.

In the kitchen, she took a good handful of her pills, which were absolutely essential for her health. As she returned them to the fridge, where the pills must be kept, she tried to remember what it was like before she had started using them. It was a hard life, before the pills. Hard life, soft everything else. It seemed she had occupied a kind of haze, on the periphery of things with her soft puppyish flesh. Her fat face. Her doughiness everywhere and her awful bowels. Yeah, the pills were the greatest thing that had ever happened to her.

She had a shower, applying her special body scrub liberally, along with scorching hot water. Long after she was dry, even after applying her cream, she felt flushed with heat – as though it was emanating from her bones.

Naked on her clean sheets, she checked her work emails.

RE: Firmwide Announcement

Hey *Retard*! WTF?

Of course I remember you!

"You're an inspiration."

Are you *finally* pitching something to me, now that I have even more power?

J

P.S.: You better say, 'Yes I am pitching something...'

RE: Firmwide Announcement

Yes, I guess it was a pitch. I don't exactly know what for.

It was also true – you are an inspiration. So there! ;)

Best

R

Whoosh. Then nothing. Until a calendar entry from someone she has never heard of.

> **Roger Chu has invited you to 'Sniff of the big time. NY OFFICE' on Friday at 11:00 UET**
>
> **Do you accept?**
>
> | I accept | I decline |

Rachel reached out and clicked 'I accept'.

As she fell into her sleep, millions of tiny, microscopic, vampire alien worm-like creatures emerged from the dietary pills she had swallowed and joined their family who were already there, happily alive inside her gut. Together, they squelched and burped and languished in her digestive system. Waiting.

On the inside, the Broadway New York office was painfully similar to the Bank Street London office. Rachel had been driven in a staff Chrysler from JFK directly to the Broadway site, there had been no chance to explore. From the little she saw, peeping from between the groaning traffic, and standing briefly on the street before entering the building, she had to agree with what everyone said about New York. It was exactly like on TV. It was yellow cabs and lights, and friendly people using their whole body to move the air as they passed you on the street. It was hotdogs and Comme des Garçons and the sound of shoes, somewhere, thousands of shoes trotting out jazz lines under the traffic.

Rachel had been directed to take the elevator to the

executive office suite on the twenty-third floor. Now she was looking at the Joan of Arc face of Jocilyn Haggus, the Debuchy silk of Jocilyn Haggus's shirt, and the Calcutta Des Amores Gecko necklace that slugged languidly between Jocilyn Haggus's two breasts.

'Jesus. You look younger than you did in Shanghai,' said Rachel. 'That was like seven years ago! Sorry. I seem unable to edit myself.'

Amazed and dazzled by the youth of this woman, and the luxury of her executive office, Rachel took a step towards Jocilyn, to look for flaws in her skin. There was nothing. She was like an infant made out of percaline.

'You look so young!' she said again, now beginning to sound more than a little bit like an idiot.

'I feel it!' said Jocilyn Haggus. 'You know what else? I'm going to pay you a compliment now, Rachel. Come with me over here to this mirror.'

Rachel crossed the office and now she was looking in a mirror that had been handmade by the renowned Venetian glass-blower Cosmo Benetolli in the late eighteenth century. Rachel knew this because it was included in the VP pages for Jocilyn Haggus on StafBoard, the HR system. Everything about Jocilyn Haggus's StafBoard page was devastatingly impressive.

Jocilyn walked behind Rachel, she rested her hands on Rachel's shoulders. Rachel saw herself in the mirror with Jocilyn behind her, putting her lips very close to the skin on Rachel's neck.

Rachel was looking sweaty, but also glowing. She was not degraded like in London mirrors. She was not blotched.

'This mirror is incredible!'

'It's not the mirror, Rachel,' said Jocilyn, touching

Rachel in different places. 'It's you. It's you in New York. This town loves you!'

'I've only just got off the plane,' laughed Rachel. 'I'm wearing long johns and compression stockings.'

'Yeah, and look at you. Have you ever, be honest, in all your life felt so much like you want to fuck yourself?'

'No,' said Rachel. 'But I have sort of never felt that way.'

Jocilyn laughed a huge New York laugh. 'Rachel. Shut up for a minute. Tell me, what do you want in life?'

'Well –'

'No. Don't do it straight away. I don't want your blurty Britsy bullshit, 'K? I want to know what you want – right down in the burn of your heart. Can you hear me? In the fire of your heart.'

Rachel took a deep breath and said, 'I want to create a line of designer blankets that are also clothes? And I want people to wear them in the most achingly young and cool places in the coldest corners of the world. I want people to look at the kids wearing my blankets and I want them to wish they were dead because they will never, ever be so damned sexy and young. I want it to be called SLUGS and have a logo that people cannot think about without sighing.'

'Jesus fucking Christ, you're ridiculous. Come on, I'm taking you to the Hot Plate.'

They went across town in another firm Chrysler. Rachel forgot about her compression stockings and looked out of the window at the glinting lights of Broadway, then Wall Street and then places she did not know or understand, but recognized from films and television programmes.

'Hey. Have some of this. It'll help you out,' said Jocilyn. Rachel was about to decline, when she noticed that she was not being offered drugs, but just a hand full of her normal diet pills. Only these looked slightly different, they were blue. The insides seemed to be swirling.

'Ah! You don't remember, then?' said Jocilyn.

'Remember what?'

'The advice I gave you all those years ago. It was the pills. Take these, take them and you will stop being such a saggy fuckface.'

'Oh! I do remember!' said Rachel, and then they were eating pills and sitting right next to each other, which was fine, and the leather on the chairs was fine too, and all of it was fine, just dandy.

It was wonderful until Jocilyn leaned over to her, across the table in the restaurant and said: 'You really are a tardigrade, you know that? That's how come you're such a successful designer now. We put tardigrades in those pills, and they control you now. Is that OK?'

They were in a restaurant, and Rachel did not remember going inside, but everything was very black, except she could see candles at all the tables, but no faces, only Jocilyn and the candle lighting her.

'What did you say, Jocilyn? What was that about tardigrades?'

'I said, don't worry about it! Let's get some air!'

They were outside on the streets of New York, in a place called TriBeCa and Rachel saw that there were people, young people, sitting outside in the warm evening drinking beer and smoking – a lot of them were smoking – and drinking coffee. A lot of them were unbearably beautiful.

'Don't they look smoking hot?' said Jocilyn.

'They are seriously hot,' said Rachel. She felt drunk. On a billboard was a huge sign that said *SLUGS*.

'Jocilyn,' Rachel said. 'How long have I been here?'

The answer, Jocilyn explained, was eighteen months. She had secured financing for her design company, and now she was pretty much running an entire department in the firm, while also putting out fashionable wearable blankets for young sexy people.

She was a tardigrade. The tardigrades were operating her life for her. She no longer needed to do anything.

'Except,' said Jocilyn, coming into focus, and now screaming at Rachel. 'You do have to speak, Rachel. You do have to speak to us, or we can't help you.'

Rachel was back in the office on the phone, and the tardigrades were going insane in her stomach. Picking up the vibrations of her bones. The headset of the phone was almost too much to endure, her new nervous system was rioting. She was an exposed gland.

'Hello?'

'H – h – h – h –'

'Hi, have we got you? Who's on the call?'

'I'm here.'

'Hi Paul.'

'We've got Oli.'

'Hi Oli.'

'And Rachael.'

'Hi Rachel.'

'H – h – hi who's that?'

'It's Theo. sorry to be so long coming back to you. So, shall we move towards the retrograde testing?'

'Theo?'

'Rachel? Tell me how are the infest tabulation margins coming along?'

'The infest...?'

'The infestation, Rachel. The retrograde.'

'Come on, Rach. You've been so formal recently. All through this call.'

'Can you describe how you feel?'

'I'm trying to reach out.'

'Yes.'

'There has been a strong need for me to, I don't know, diversify?'

'Yes, just reach out when you feel something like the need to diversify.'

'I feel something like the need to diversify.'

And she was surrounded by gold light, forming baubles and floating, peacock-tailing, through the open plan air.

Then there came a cold sensation, within her gold blindness as she reached and squirmed and froze and atrophied, the feeling of someone saying, maybe very, very distantly:

'Wrap her up. Get her in a blanket she can wear this blanket. She is terribly, oh, I mean look at her. Be careful, she's been voted One to Watch recently. But, for God's sake. Just look how she stands there with her mouth open, like she's at a spin class.'

MOTHER'S DAY CARD FROM A WOODEN OBJECT

Mother!

At an unusual time of year, and in an impractical format, this card is to say thank you (again) for raising me. I realise it's a recurring theme with me lately, especially since it is now clear to us both that we have had our last foreign holiday. You've tossed me affectionately into the back of the car for the final time.

It has not been easy raising a wooden object as if it were a human child. Not even a human-shaped wooden object.

In this card, which I cannot actually write, but I know you will somehow understand that I intended to be written, I want to acknowledge that.

As you recall, I arrived in the passenger seat of your brown, Scandinavian-manufactured car around the end of spring in the mid 1980s. As the traffic had slowed, you were taking a moment to gaze at something out of the window. It was probably a dirty sign, or an empty packet of Maltesers as it skittered along the gutter.

And when you turned back, there I was: a helpless lump of wood that you had to accept, in that moment, as your son. You continued driving, very slightly more confidently than before. You were a mother now.

There were no booties or onesies or teddies. There were no balloons in the hospital ward, or flowers on the kitchen table. There was just you and me, in the brown car at the intersection between Windy Arbour and Spring Lane.

Thank you for bearing the humiliation of enrolling me in the reception class at the local school. I remember the head mistress, who was very fond of the colour green. You entered her office carrying me under your arm. She asked you to sit on a tiny chair. For me, there was the carpet. It had a map of a town on it, with a wide road running past all the shops, and the hospital and the fire station and the police station.

As the head mistress looked from you on your little chair, to me, an abstract shape of dark wood on the rug, you explained how things were.

When the headmistress asked, you told her that you did not know what type of wood I was, and that you wouldn't be making any effort to find out. 'What am I going to do? Get him tested? I will not get him tested,' you said. 'He's got rights, free will and he needs an education. He won't disrupt the lesson, and he won't take up a desk,' you said. You ended the whole thing with a tight nod and a flat smile, which I had seen you practice in the mirror.

Throughout your chat with the head mistress, I remained on the rug, tracking the shape of the road, enjoying the way the sun came through the high iron-framed windows into the room.

Just as you promised, I was a quiet pupil, and I did not take up any room. At parents' evenings, you assured that same head mistress – in her grass-green pullover, with her coils of quite luscious black hair – that I had shown every sign of learning. 'I have the absolute conviction,' you said, 'that he can read his own name, that he understands the basics of addition and subtraction.' You thanked the school for their continued commitment to the education of all.

At home, it was alright. There wasn't any money, but it was alright because it was just us. And even though you sometimes said, 'I wonder where your father is!' or 'Why isn't he here sorting this mess out?' we both knew exactly where he was. His phone number was written on the first page of the almost empty address book that we kept next to the phone.

Mother, do you remember when the freezer broke in the middle of the night and we had to put our towels down to sop up the mess? It was our own freezer – the landlord had originally objected, preferring to let the property with a freezer in it that he had tested and had a warranty for. But you had insisted. That freezer had been your most valuable wedding gift, and you still clung to my father's assertion that it would never die, that it was of such a superior brand that it would go on and on. 'If we have kids,' you remembered him saying, 'we'll be able to pass it down, and our kids can pass it down to our grandkids.'

But when it broke and you called him in the dead of night, he was confused, baffled that you had held onto that old piece of junk all this time. 'God,' he said. 'I thought you'd have skipped that fucking thing by now.'

You remained calm, asking him to focus on the fact we needed his help.

'Just tell the landlord,' he said.

And you tried to explain that no, it wasn't the landlord's responsibility. 'I need some practical help please,' you said to him.

There were long silences. He insisted that you stay on the line while he looked up the rules and regulations concerning white goods in tenancy agreements.

Meanwhile, you replaced the sodden towels one-handed, the phone cradled in the crook of your neck.

'What are we going to do with all this?' you whispered to yourself, as you ferried trays of defrosting food to the counter. 'How the fuck are we going to pay...'

While Dad umm'd and ah'd and looked for old letters he had regarding this exact situation, you put all the rapidly defrosting sausages into the oven. More than twenty of them, on two trays, with the determination that you could easily live on cold sausage sandwiches at work for weeks. You told me, over and over again, what you would say about it to the people in the office. 'They'll just have to live with it,' you said. 'If they complain about the smell of sausages. What's wrong with sausage sandwiches for God's sake?' You went on muttering to yourself in the dark kitchen, cursing people I did not know. Cursing your job, too, and the people in the office.

Dad hung up and called back a few minutes later. He was breathing heavily and he said he would call the landlord on your behalf since you couldn't manage it yourself, and you screamed. You shouted, 'Don't call the fucking landlord! I have explained about the landlord. It's not his freezer.'

You told Dad not to do anything. That calling him had been a waste of time. That you were tired.

And then I could just hear him saying, 'No – I'll tell you what's a waste of fucking time...' but there was no more before you left the room with the phone and his voice was gone.

I looked at the sausages through the little greasy window in the oven door until you came back in, and both your voices – yours and Dad's – were softer, though still strained.

You spoke to Dad on and off throughout that night, do you remember? And I tried not to look too much like I was in the way while you mopped up the liquid and chased softening peas across the linoleum.

Dad eventually said that the inevitable conclusion was that you would have to buy a new freezer in the morning. 'Get it on credit,' he said. 'Just get something sorted and leave me out of it.' He said he had done everything in his power to help. Then he hung up. You slammed the phone onto the counter and took a breath.

I decided not to allude to the fact that Dad hadn't mentioned me once.

Thank you, though, mother because there were much happier times to come. For example, thank you for taking me on my date with Sarah. Thank you for sitting in her living room and placing me on the end of the sofa nearest to where Sarah was sitting. Thank you for explaining to Sarah, twelve, that I was really interested in her personality and that I liked the way she laughed. Thank you for telling her that I really liked the Blur T-shirt she was wearing, and that I had my eye on a Suede one, which I had seen recently in a shop in Coventry.

As we left, you remarked on how odd you found it that anyone would allow a woman with a lump of wood to sit in their living room and say all these things to their daughter. Who would tolerate it? you said. There must be something wrong with her family. I partly agreed, but I also really liked Sarah for sitting through it all, and for smiling at me three times while you spoke. I do think you could have given her more credit for trying to make you a cup of tea, before you realised she had never made one before, and decided to step in.

I had no answer for you when you asked where her parents had been at the time.

Perhaps you're wondering why I have chosen this moment to send this card – which, as you know, I cannot actually send or write in a physical sense because I am entirely made from wood.

Well, as I'm sure you can understand, I have reached an age where I find myself succumbing to certain feelings of desperation regarding the future. This is not the same as that time I allowed myself to be carted away by your artist friend – although I was pretty low then, too. You probably won't recall.

He intended to use me as the material from which to make a carving of a fabulous head. Did you know about that? Our artist friend? I thought he must have told you. Maybe not.

He was intending to carve this head using techniques derived from the ancient Saxon craft of totem making. He would use the head as a way of expressing something – he did not yet know exactly what – about his own failures in the eyes of his very masculine brother. The choice of wood, he said, was very important. It represented the unswerving, unemotional force, and yet he would hack into it, he said, in an intentionally brutal way. This would, he hoped, result in a final shape that felt wounded or ashamed. I was really looking forward to being mutilated in this way. I did not fear the pain of it. I was sure, in fact, that I was incapable of physical pain in that way, because of my one-hundred percent wooden form.

I had already sustained a few chips and dents

at this time. I am heavy, and an awkward size and shape. It was inevitable that I'd get dropped a few times, even by you.

I remember how much you wept when I first slipped out of your grasp. You were getting me out of the car seat, ready to deposit me at school. We were running late because there was a shoe you couldn't find. I slipped out of your hand and cracked onto the road. I rolled a few times. You picked me up and, at a first glance, you couldn't see anything amiss. I was fine. You left me in the usual place for one of the teachers to carry inside, or if it was Bad Back Bower, I went onto the cart.

I was fine, but I saw you rubbing your eyes under your glasses as you negotiated your way back into the flow of traffic, already late for work, crying about what Wendy was going to say, and how could you explain that part of the reason was because of a shoe and the other part was because you had dropped your wooden child.

When you collected me later that day, I tried to conceal the chip, using various distraction methods I had cultivated over the years. I didn't want you to see it – you felt bad enough as it was – but just as you were finally getting ready to sit down and eat a meal, I dropped my guard and you saw what had happened to me.

You lowered your fork from your mouth. 'The one good thing about today,' you said, 'has been the prospect of my sausage and chips.' At the time, sausage and chips was your favourite food. You liked to dip the chips in mayonnaise, which in those days hardly any English people were doing. 'I have been looking forward to this all day,' you said. 'And now there's this!' You picked me up and examined the damage, looked horrified by it.

It became one of our bad nights. The food went uneaten, hard and cold within the hour. Why hadn't I allowed you to know about the dent in my body? you wanted to know. Why were you being made to feel like this in your own home? 'If you get hurt again,' you said, 'tell me, for God's sake, otherwise what is the fucking point in any of this!'

I said nothing, because I was made of wood. Even if I had been able to speak, I would not have known how to say that the chip was only superficial and did not hurt, and that what was really painful was knowing that I would never be able to make life any better, that I would always be susceptible to chips and cracks. There was never going to be anything anyone could do to change that.

So it was, with this knowledge that superficial damage didn't hurt me, that in a moment of adolescent foolishness and angst, I contrived to allow myself to be in the pile of logs and other timber artefacts you had prepared for your artist friend. Of course, he noticed straight away that it was your son he was about to hack into with all his available masculine rage.

For a moment, I saw him contemplate how much more powerful his work would be if he carved it from the wooden object that his friend obsessively called her child. It was only the briefest of moments, and yet it seemed to stretch out into minutes and maybe even hours. In the end, he drove me home, all the while he was saying how good it was to see me and how sorry he was for his mistake, and he invited me to play cricket that weekend with himself and his two daughters, who were, he thought, probably about the same age as me.

He tried to make them involve me in the game. It was sweet – 'Here, you can be wicket keeper.' – and then cheering as the ball bounced off my wooden form back onto the stumps. It was all rather sweet and rather desperate. He felt very sorry for you, and for us. His daughters too, but they needn't have.

I've always just been a piece of wood – I never needed to come to terms with my form. I did not have to learn to love the contours that make up my 'back' – resonant of driftwood, but much richer in colour, much heavier and harder to the touch. I am proud of my grain. Is that a phrase? Perhaps it could be, just between the two of us. Or even in the real world.

'He's proud of his grain,' you could say. You could say it about someone else, something unconnected with me, and people would know what you meant.

I'm saying all this because you might have worried that I was writing this card out of desperation – that I can no longer cope with being just a piece of wood. But I feel no desperation about being made of wood. I am wood, so it's fine.

But you are right, there is a sort of desperation in my urge to write this card. The desperation I'm referring to is not about me, but actually more connected to the fact that I am haunted by visions of your death. I see you frail. I see you alone – the dog has died long ago. I see the world we inhabit close in around you. I go for days sometimes, under a tea-towel you have casually chucked onto me, and then reel with self-loathing as I see the inevitable shock and sadness on your face when you peel away the cloth and realise how many days it has been since you left me like this.

I see you leafing through old school reports – which my teachers had indulgently written for you, to humour you, you have always assumed, with news of the progress of your entirely wood-based child. For example: 'We really feel as if he is grasping the finer details of the Tudor age' or 'His intended course work is above average, if a little ambitious.'

I see you leafing through these things and letting them slip from your fingers and drop to the floor, before you either fall asleep there on the chair, or rouse yourself with a snort and go into the other room to look at spreadsheets for work. You have worked so hard, Mother. You have worked so long. But you always say, you only remember the rests. You only remember the lovely holidays.

Do you remember? We could barely afford it. We had to suffer, you always said, whenever we had anything nice. And so it was, we would come home to unexpected bills, and something would break and we would have to suffer for the bit of sun we had had.

I really want to thank you for those holidays. I want you to know that they were worth it. Worth it for the people we met. The other tourists who you found it so easy to talk to – who indulged us both by allowing me my own sunbed. And, in order to give you some well-earned privacy, the hotels that indulged us by allowing me to have my own room, with a view over the village.

My son is a wooden object, you would say. But he must have his privacy.

How I loved to look out of my window and watch those hot surfaces cooling in the dusk air, the sound of Mediterranean voices floating like music, and the smell of salt and loud fresh seafood.

I can still recall how it felt to be in that hotel room early one morning when the cleaner came in. I remember the way he sat at the little desk, set a timer on his watch – the exact allocation of time allowed for each room - and took off his shoes. He lent back in the chair and breathed out heavily. He did not look at me when he spoke.

'I've heard about you,' he said. 'You don't deserve any of this. Do you? Are you really getting anything out of this? You are a lump of wood. You have a better life than I can give my family. Do you think that's ok? Of course, you don't have an opinion. You're not a human being.'

'You said it,' I said. Although of course he could not hear me.

He took off his socks and massaged his feet. 'Your mother is a good person,' he said. 'She told me not to bother cleaning. She gave me a nice tip. I think she might be an angel,' he said. All the time he was talking, he was massaging his feet, balling up little sausages of black lint which he discarded carefully into the waste paper bin.

He complained about his socks. 'They make us wear these things. I can see why; this uniform isn't going to look good without the right black socks. I don't pay for them, but I know they pay me less each hour to cover the cost of the socks. Look how they fall apart. I have this black fluffy shit all over my bed at home, when I get home late and don't have time to rub it all off. I usually try to have a shower before I go to bed.'

Then he stood up, quite abruptly, and walked across the room to where I was by the window. He undid his belt and pulled down his trousers and pants. Then he lay his thick white penis along my 'back', like he was placing a fish on a chopping board. I heard his camera snap on his phone.

He didn't say anything else as he put everything back on and left my room.

I'm wood though, so really it didn't bother me.

But anyway, as I said, all of this has come from a sense of desperation, in a way, a dislike of watching you fade. Watching them come and install hand-rails so you can stay in your home (yet another unwanted concession from yet another despairing landlord who regrets housing us) with only limited outside assistance.

'There's no one who can come?' The assessment officer asked. 'It says here, you have a son. Does he live far away?'

You gestured to the area where I am nestled, forgotten for a few weeks beside a plate with dried pickle on it, amongst the other living room ornaments. At first the assessment officer didn't understand, but you calmly explained, through the now constant fog of your age, that I am your son, but I am made entirely from wood. I am not even human shaped.

The assessment officer seemed very interested in our story and so she stayed an extra hour to ask about us, completely oblivious to how tired it made you to answer those questions.

'You have very philosophical views,' the assessment officer said. 'You have a very philosophical outlook,' she said. 'I spend all day out and about, meeting people, and there aren't a lot of times I want to hear more. People think they're unique because of their circumstance,' she said. 'But it's the most normal thing in the world, needing help. It's the most ordinary thing. People think they are extraordinary because they are surrounded by love, but human beings will love anything,' the assessment officer said.

A long time ago, you would have taken issue with that sentiment. But now you don't. Now, you let her go on.

I could not interject. I could not suddenly rise up and say, 'I think my mother has had enough now.'

'But,' you said, breakingly, abruptly, 'I am not surrounded by love. I do not want to be surrounded by anything.'

You said that what has kept you going all this time is waiting, just waiting, for wisps. 'Wisps are enough,' you said.

The assessment officer asked you to elaborate, insisting on making you talk more, even though your voice had become audibly raw.

You said that in the beginning, in that first winter, you had discovered that I had been left in the cold, near the back door in the kitchen, on a stone tile. I was visibly smaller, you said, because of the cold. You had immediately rushed me inside and put me a safe distance from the fire. You wrapped your arms around me. In those few minutes, you felt the wood that I am made of swell back to my normal size, and very slightly beyond.

'I felt him breathe,' you said. You turned to me, beside the pickle-stained plate, and you said, 'I felt you breathe.'

You told me, and the assessment officer, that these things are enough. 'You can live a hundred years,' you said, 'on just that fractional breath.'

☺ IF YES, PLEASE EXPLAIN
YOUR ANSWER ☺

It's simply that I feel very supported in my role. I know my role. I know that when there is hardship it is temporary and will ultimately be rewarded.

☺ What single thing would improve our workplace? ☺

An egg arrives one day. The egg is about the size of an unused roll of kitchen paper. It is Manuel who brings the egg into the office.

When I ask Manuel about the egg, he says it was delivered to his home address with instructions to carefully bring it to work. There was no name or address for the sender, he says.

The egg instantly changes the atmosphere in the office. Our individual preoccupations dissipate. The lingering dispute about how to label the portfolio wall is forgotten.

The political differences between the Product and Commerce teams are put on ice.

I am deeply attracted to the egg. I find that my breath changes significantly when I am close enough to see the texture of the shell. I do some research and conclude that the egg causes me to reach an instant Alpha brainwave state. I am relaxed and focused, and have total clarity. I feel an energy that is close to sexual, but is not actually sexual.

I am not alone in my feelings. The egg becomes a common focus of all our down time.

The egg itself seems to go through changes in pattern and texture. It is green at times, depending on the light, and at other times it is lilac with pale cream. These colours move and fluctuate during changes of the light and times of day, and also, weather conditions.

We gather to admire the egg frequently. At first, gathering around Manuel's desk before it is moved to the reception area where there is better access. We stand sometimes in a wide arc, finger-to-finger around the egg, hardly breathing.

The texture of the shell, the shade of its tepid green and the counter-shade of its mournful lilac.

We stand for hours.

But we are not idle in our work.

We are aware that the egg contains an animal, and that this animal has a future beyond its egg state. We are responsible for whatever hatches out, and we are all invigorated by this sense of responsibility in a primal way.

As a parent, I feel an especially strong duty of care to the animal inside the egg. I think often about holding it, and helping it to feed. Cleaning up its warm shit and piss.

We do not know what will come out of the egg, but all of us have our suspicions.

I don't talk to anyone about my own expectations. I feel reluctant in case I get into a disagreement about the physical appearance of the animal. I worry that someone else's prediction might taint my own.

For example, I find it impossible to countenance certain types of animal coming out of the egg. I cannot even think about it being a lizard, or something like that.

I am convinced that it will be a special bird. I do not know in what way it will be special. I can't seem to pin down what I think its personality will be.

One day I picture a spectacular coot, all butch and florid, getting up in your face. Other days it is a very calm egret, with a clever smile and a gentle *crrp crrp* call.

When not daydreaming about the egg, I work harder than ever. We all do. There is an immense feeling of common purpose in the whole company. I feel emotionally closer my colleagues. It's as though we understand each other better, now we have a tangible focus, beyond the success of the company.

As time goes on, and still avoiding specific details, I talk to people about the egg's progress. It becomes, maybe, my thing. I bring up the subject with people quite openly, and they seem happy to share their feelings with me, within a few unspoken parameters.

For example, Coventry Chris says he feels good when he is alone with the egg. He says that sometimes he can even hear music playing. When I press him to tell me what the music is like, he cannot answer. He just closes his eyes and moves his head as if in rapture to something slow moving. He makes small jazz-motivated gestures.

After an awkward conversation with a nosy delivery person, I put forward an 'all-hands' suggestion that the reception area might not be the most suitable space to incubate the egg. Apart from our shared horror at the idea of a delivery person nudging the egg, or even looking at it, I feel as though more could be done to help the incubation process.

It is agreed that we must all look after the egg, taking a shift each, to ensure that whatever is inside is kept stable and healthy.

During our incubation shift, we are allowed to improvise, and do what comes naturally to help nurture the egg.

My method is to clutch the egg between my knees. I have very strong thigh and calf muscles. I am able to walk with the egg tucked up there at a fairly good speed. I also squat regularly when there are atmospheric changes, in order to sustain a regular temperature.

I am grateful to Gilly Beraldry, who draws on her extensive yoga knowledge to advise me on the tension levels I should place on the egg. She shows me that, by inverting the egg, I can use my knees as a steadying prop, rather than rely on pressure and friction to grip the shell.

In week eight of the incubation period, when everything is in full swing and we are full of positivity, I arrive at work to find a grey-faced Manuel. Something has gone wrong with the egg, he says. It has gone cold.

I go to look. The sight of the egg depresses me instantly. I feel a profound sense of loss and despair.

The shell appears shrunken and dreadful. It is coated in a kind of moss which leaves a gravelly residue on my hand when I touch it.

The feeling of the gravelly residue makes me feel sweaty and unsafe.

A meeting is instantly called in the board room. We all pile in. Dieter Laborio, who is the one on incubation duty, places the sad, cold egg on the table.

We scrutinise the egg.

The agenda of this meeting is:

- Did someone's method fail?
- Has the egg been dropped?
- What can be done?
- We do not place blame on Dieter Laborio.
- Is this real?
- Next steps.

After the meeting, we each have an agreed action. We cannot do anything except try to care for the egg as we were before, but now we have entered a form of hypercare mode.

We call it: Hypercare Mode.

Instead of improvised strategies and innovations for incubating the egg, we decide to create a Zone Of Nurturing and Enrichment (ZONE).

In teams, we assemble around the heat lamp which has been moved from the reception area to the break-out room – this is where the ZONE is established.

The egg is placed within a crest of bean bags that have been partially split and adapted into a loosely constructed mega-bag.

Stray polystyrene beads and other insulation materials that make a mess are managed through an almost constant sweeping, preening and remixing regime.

Someone takes a dry string mop and sweeps the stray beads and other fibres into a loose, long pile. The pile is then silently moved to the edge of the crest and the beads and fibres are remixed, back into the general incubation material.

The sweeping and preening regime is partially my idea, and I am proud when one of the senior team remarks on its beneficial meditative properties as an activity, beyond its primary function of keeping the ZONE tidy and safe.

We take it in turns to monitor the egg in the ZONE. Some shifts are evening-to-night. We must all take at least one of these per month.

My first evening-to-night watch in the ZONE is with Manuel. I feel especially excited about being there with Manuel. His love of the egg is widely regarded as the most pure because he was the one who received the egg at his home address, and then brought it in to the office. His natural happy nature, his sunshine personality, makes him a likable figure for this role in the egg's life. It is difficult to resent Manuel's special affinity.

Manuel is a great authority on the health of the egg. He is swollen with hope, he says at the start of our shift. He is filled with renewed joy.

The egg is making good progress again. The moss of sadness has dried up and crumbled off.

I confess to Manuel that I took some of the dried moss home and mixed it into my bath water to see if it has revitalising effects.

Manuel tells me he feels that the problems were actually a natural part of the egg's process. He isn't surprised that the moss has made me look and feel younger and more vigorous.

After my chat with Manuel, I feel a great sense of peace. I have a chilled out conversation with the delivery person as I receive the pizza.

I too am filled with renewed joy as I open the pizza, cut the slices into more distinct slices, and pour drinks for the two of us. Everything, every tiny action is calm and has a ritualistic quality. I tell Manuel that before the egg there was only a void.

'What about your kids, dude?'

'A void,' I say.

Manuel cannot tell if I'm joking. Even when I reassure him that, of course, my kids aren't a void.

'In fact,' I say to Manuel, 'all I have been able to feel is an intense kind of gratitude recently. Specifically, in relation to my kids.'

I tell him that everything makes me thankful. I'm even thankful on a crowded bus, which has nowhere for me to sit, and nowhere for my children to sit, and is occupied by bad people who are selfish and have no respect. 'Even in this situation,' I say, 'I am grateful. I have nothing to be sad about because, in the end, the bus still takes us where we want to go.'

'That's very cool, man,' Manuel says.

'Yeah man!' I say. 'I feel that I can choose to have a problem with it, or I can hold my children close to me and tell them how wonderful it's going to be at the park or the café or the bookshop.'

Manuel says he knows what I mean.

'What about you, Man?' I ask. 'How do you feel now that there is the egg?'

Manuel tells me that his feeling towards the egg is so specific that he actually cannot put it into English or Spanish words.

Unable to speak, he goes into a kind of trance. His eyebrows are fixed in a raised position, as though he has been startled by some profoundly sad news. I can tell that he has entered a Theta state brainwave pattern, so I put a hoody round his shoulders and sweep the area for stray beads and other fibres until the morning.

The hatching occurs in silence.

The animal is hard for each of us to describe accurately. We continue using indirect sentiments to express our love for the animal, just as we did when it was inside the egg.

For example, instead of, 'I love her great green eyes,' I say, 'I love the way she looks at you,' because this is less controversial and is not open to debate about the animal's exact physical appearance.

Instead of saying, 'He has lovely soft hair,' I say, 'I love to just stroke him.'

We manage to negotiate pronoun assumptions well enough. The animal seems to identify differently from colleague to colleague, and we don't pick fights when someone seems to have got it 'wrong'.

Me and Manuel organise a spontaneous naming ceremony meeting in the ZONE.

In the meeting, Manuel leads a glorifying chant. The animal is given the name Tritty.

During the first three months after Tritty's hatching, we each spend one night per month sitting up with her. We do this in shifts, continuing the timetable we had settled into when she was in the egg.

Soon, Tritty is old enough to move by herself. Tritty's ZONE becomes more like a kindergarten.

I have a good time in there, playing skatch and hoop-head with Tritty. She is, it turns out, neither Coot nor Egret. I don't know what she is at this stage, but I feel deep love and responsibility for her.

Of course, I regularly question the reality of what is happening. I ask myself if it can really be the case that Manuel brought in this egg, and we hatched it, and I go home later and later each day, suffering the misery of my children becoming ever-more distant, and the anguish of lying to my partner about how much pressure I am under at work, when actually, I am not under any pressure at all. In fact, I am giving real love to an animal that came from an egg.

I am a success in my role. I am nailing my work. I have new ideas for ways to improve all the time. All of us are shining. It's an amazing time.

Tritty goes away one morning,
and we worry when we can't find him.

Then he appears while we're eating in the communal area.

Tritty is swathed in a gown that covers all of his features. He is carrying an object. He bears the object above his head.

The object itself is about the size and depth of a quite chunky school blazer badge. Tritty bears it to the central clearing in the communal eating space. He stands in the middle of the floor, the spot where the founders make announcements during the monthly town hall meetings.

We break away from our chit-chat, quietly tidy away all signs of food, and gather in a kind of reverential arc around Tritty.

From among us, Sophie is chosen. Tritty motions for Sophie to come forward, which she does with a lowered head. Tritty's slow movements become injected with a clear and distinct purpose. He raises up the object towards Sophie. Sophie receives the object ceremonially, with her head bowed and her hands thrust upwards. She receives the object in a way that can only be instinctive because none of this has been choreographed. Until a few moments before this ceremony, all of us were just eating lunch.

And so, Sophie is the first of us to receive a talisman. Many of us expected it to be Manuel.

'I'm sorry, man,' I say to him.

He doesn't react. He observes Sophie and her talisman. He observes Tritty bootling about, ignoring Manuel, as if he is nobody special.

After that first talisman ceremony, Tritty's physical development accelerates. Soon she has a clear vocal range, and the power of speech. Adam P. is the first to report that he has had an actual two-way conversation with Tritty.

He tells us that, thanks to Tritty, he is more aware of certain trappings and pitfalls in his life.

Tritty makes more talismans and we each receive one. All of us repeat or create our own version of Sophie's mannered acceptance style.

Each ceremony is the same as the last one. It is repetitive and yet not even slightly boring to watch. The ceremonial feeling of being given a talisman loses none of its potency.

Across the company, love for Tritty grows.

Our productivity increases. Relationships with clients and new leads seem effortless.

Software problems appear to resolve themselves.

My talisman is a burnt webbing that represents 'The Shadow of The Pinnacle'. I am also aware of a new motto to live by, given to me by Tritty. My motto is, 'The rain outside the window has passed.'

Concepts like the 'Shadow of The Pinnacle', and mottos like mine, enter our lives organically, without any of us realising it is happening. Each of us is given two or three concepts to treasure, as well as the talisman.

Like living conceptual tarot cards, they can be characters, or, more accurately, figurines. Some figurines are:

The demon of the fever of the slowness

The cruiser

Hallowed children

Energetic mow woman

Some people are bestowed moods too, sometimes referred to as energies:

Absorption

No longer hungering

Hawk sounding plaza time

Billion airs

Children at play in the yard no longer haunt your sweet aunt

Each mood or figurine is open to interpretation only by the person upon whom it is bestowed. If you want to ask someone what their mood or figurine means, you have to do it outside of working hours, in a safe space for both of you. You have to be aware that it is deeply personal, and you may hear something unsettling or disruptive to your world view. If you feel uncomfortable with this, it's best not to ask.

The general feeling is that Tritty unites us without a unifying text. We do not need to pry into another person's *Hawk sounding plaza time* or know the qualities of their *Laughing sound going into a nest.*

As the rituals come to an end, and we all have our talismans, Tritty's routine becomes quite fixed. He generally appears during working hours only. He bimbles about, nodding appreciatively, giving each of us a few seconds of his time. A bit like a judge on that TV programme about baking. But instead of baking, it's software development.

Soon, there are no Tritty appearances at all after six p.m. This suits us all because we agree that we can't really take Tritty out in public, and we like to go for an after-work drink pretty regularly.

A few of us are in a bar when I notice that Manuel looks low in spirits.

'Hey Manuel,' I say. 'What's the big deal? You know, you look super unhappy.'

And Manuel says, 'Yeah something's been bothering me for a while.'

He whispers his words because he doesn't want the

conversation to become too public. I scooch round the table to be next to him.

'Tell me, my friend. What's up?'

Manuel hunches his shoulders, he moves away as I touch him on the shoulder. He is absolutely ice cold. Painfully cold to the touch. I don't mention it, in case it throws him off.

'Well, actually,' he says, 'before I tell you anything, man, I want to be sure you're not going to judge me too hard for it.'

'No way! I'm not gonna do that to you, Manuel. You're my friend, as well as my colleague. You know? I will never judge you. You brought us Tritty!'

'Well,' he says. 'To tell you the truth, I find Tritty to be a problem. All of you have been thriving, but to me, Tritty is ugly and makes me sad. I never thought I would miss a fucking egg so badly.'

Manuel's words are tough for me to hear, but I do not react.

'OK. Tell me, Manuel, what was your talisman?'

'Sorrowful water passing by in silence,' says Manuel.

'Oh yeah. I remember,' I say. It's beautiful. It's like you, Manuel. It's so powerful, like a force of nature. But also, with great integrity.'

'Yeah.'

We sit for a while in silence because, at this stage, it has become the custom between colleagues to have a repeated conversation in which the one speaking about their talisman describes how amazing it makes them feel. But it doesn't seem like that can happen. Manuel is not taking his part in it.

He sits and he looks unbearably glum. He seems cold enough to freeze water.

'I find Tritty hideous,' he spits suddenly. 'Tritty is an ugly, sleazy curse in our lives.'

I am shocked, but I stay calm. 'But Manuel! What about the good things that have been happening since Tritty came along?'

'It's a coincidence.'

I say, 'I can tell this is causing you a lot of pain to talk this way. I hate to see you suffering.'

'Tritty is all over me!' he says, spittle forming at the sides of his mouth. 'He is on me whenever we are alone. His skin is like a wet spoon.'

I don't disclose this, but I find it amazing to hear about Manuel's physical contact with Tritty. I have never touched Tritty, and never seen anyone else make physical contact.

Manuel tells me how like dead skin Tritty feels. How like a rubbery, cold eel, tense and evil under his touch. He tells me that he thinks Tritty belongs in a lab and we should tell the government.

I manage to convince Manuel not to tell the government about Tritty, and in return I agree to talk with Tritty and explain how Manuel feels, and try to find a path to a resolution.

I head back to the office building. I tell Saint Holland, the night security guard, that I have left something unfinished in the office. I tell him the name of the company and show my card.

Saint Holland doesn't mind. He's got his book, so if it's all the same, he says he won't accompany me up in the lift, as he would normally.

As the office lights flicker into life, I call to Tritty in my unique way.

Each of us has our own call, usually with actions. If there is no action, then stillness itself is an action.

Mine is slow moving. It comes with hardly a noise at all.

I lift my chin in my mind, my body becomes transformed. It's like a bird, a great albatross, or a mighty goose, kicking its beak upward. A swallowing call comes from down inside me.

Brrrrrup. Herrrrrupp.

A goose with the voice of a trilling dove. But, as I say, the sound itself is actually very faint. Sometimes it hardly catches at all. I don't say any words. It's just that sound, and perhaps because I have had some drinks, my call is especially moving to me and I am compelled to embody my call perhaps more than I would if the others were here watching.

Tritty comes mooching across the tiles of the office, looking shyly left and right, and up and down. Tritty is small, about the size of a young Labrador, but of course on two gorgeous human male legs, and with a torso covered in glittering golden feathers.

Tritty does not have a beak, but rather a somewhat crocodilian muzzle, crushed up into a stub. The colour of Tritty's stub is a deep rich peach.

'Hi Tritty,' I say. 'You know, Manuel is struggling. Is there anything we can do?'

Tritty tells me nothing. I ask if it's private.

Tritty indicates that yes, it is a private issue between him and Manuel.

But what can I do to help? You know, part of my job – a big part of my job – is about cohesion with Manuel. I also, emotionally, the idea of Manuel feeling such animosity towards you, Tritty, it just makes me – are you listening? Tritty? OK, yes. Yes. Yes.'

I say 'yes' because while I talk Tritty gazes at my talisman, interrupting my flow and demanding my attention.

I should say that in the beginning, I wore my talisman around my neck. Yet, over time, the light, ephemeral substance Tritty made it from bonded with the flesh around my sternum. In fact, every talisman Tritty makes bonds, on a molecular level, to the flesh of the wearer.

Tritty gazes at mine to remind me of its meaning. Which is, as I said, *Passing rain no longer outside the window*. It means I have to listen to my own voice. I have to listen to what I want, and not worry so much about others.

'Yes, yes Tritty. The rain has passed from outside the window. It has, but I am thinking of myself, really. I need to know what's wrong with Manuel.'

Tritty becomes evasive.

I raise my voice, just very slightly, to ask Tritty to stand still and tell me what's going on with Manuel. My raised voice is a momentary fissure, nothing more, in which I intimate to Tritty that Manuel, as a human being deserves my consideration, and that Tritty should do everything to help me.

Tritty looks at me for a long while, with a sarcastic expression on his muzzle. Then, without any warning or preparation, Tritty exposes the gentle head of a teacher.

The teacher's gentle head emerges from the plume of feathers around Tritty's throat.

It is attached by a stalk of a neck. The stalk-neck is quite weak, and the head lilts and smiles benignly.

Tritty begins moving his body about abruptly, rushing around the floor space in the ZONE, causing the gentle head of the teacher to drag along the ground.

The face of the gentle teacher looks shocked that Tritty is allowing this to happen, allowing its head to bounce painfully. It drags its teeth against the hard floor tiles.

The face of the gentle teacher has no voice. There is no breath at all in it, so the movements of the mouth make a wet clicking sound, and the inside of the mouth finishes in a shallow throat, it has about the same capacity as a small sports sock, unstretched.

I am given to understand that Tritty is proud of this behaviour.

I feel quite sick. As if all the negative feelings that Tritty helped me remove over the last few months, and during the time of the egg, have all come rushing back now with a terrible force.

'Tritty, what have you done?' I ask. 'What have you done to Manuel?'

Before Tritty can answer, I realise I am holding the heavy pole we use to open the high window in the atrium area of the office.

'What have you been doing to him?' I repeat.

Tritty tries to distract me by insinuating that the *Snow will not come again for seven years.*

I haven't got time to interpret this information properly, and I raise my voice even more loudly than before. I shout at Tritty.

'Tritty! Gentle teacher, I appeal to you too! Tell me what you did to Manuel. Tell me or else –'

I am interrupted by another voice. Not Tritty, or the gentle teacher.

'Everything alright, Ben?' says the voice. It's Saint Holland. He is standing with his legs shoulder-width apart and his back straight, in between the double doors of the lift vestibule.

With him is Kate W. from the senior team.

'Kate, I'm sorry to be here late, like this, but I saw Manuel earlier. He's sick. There's something the matter with him. He's been, I don't know the word, contaminated.'

And even though when we talked it didn't register with me, I can now picture vividly that Manuel has a substantial, festering wound on the side of his body.

'He's got a kind of infliction,' I say to Kate W. 'On his side. Like a ragged cut, and I think it came from Tritty.'

I point the pole at Tritty.

'Alright,' says Kate W. 'Well, I think the first thing that needs to happen is that you put that pole down.'

Saint Holland steps towards me. Saint Holland is not a frightening man physically. He's a student. He reads books about architecture all night and then hits the gym, mostly to work on his cardio. But he knows how to commit to the moment. He knows how to respond to a threat.

'Put it down, eh?' he says.

'I am. I am just putting it away,' I say, laughing at the pole.

There is an additional moment in which I still don't move. Nobody moves at all.

I realise that if I leave it even a second more, then I will have become a threat.

I laugh and then calmly put the pole back where it belongs, which of course involves going to the other side of the office, round where the Pre-Sales team sits.

When I return, Tritty has gone. This is very normal: Tritty does not like to see people consecutively without a break.

Kate W. is alone. She sits at one of the communal tables. She is calmer than before. The atmosphere is more relaxed. There are lamps glowing. She has poured us a drink from the Friday drinks supply.

'Sit down,' Kate says.

The way she says it reminds me of why she's one of the best people I have ever worked with. I sit down and simultaneously make that acknowledgement internally.

'I'm sorry about the way you saw me with Tritty. I wasn't going to do anything. The pole I had in my hand, was not intended for –'

'Don't worry,' Kate W says. She leans towards me, across the table. She has an earnest expression on her face. 'You are right about Manuel,' she says. 'He was wounded during a one-to-one with Tritty earlier this week. He's been keeping it a secret from everyone. Tell me, did he show you the wound?'

'No. I couldn't see it at the time. We were just talking, but now the memory of it is there, in my head. I don't know how to explain it to you. I could show you exactly where it is on his body.'

I tenderly picture Manuel. I can tell that Kate W. is doing the same. Tritty has taught us this. An exercise in which we are each able to jointly render an imagined form and explore it together with descriptions and gestures. We have used it to model data architecture. We have used it to embody a road map during presentations and internal workshops.

This is the first time we have used this technique to conjure up the actual body of a co-worker with a wound.

Kate W. wonders, 'Should we check his hands and feet? For puncture wounds?'

'No,' I say. 'Manuel isn't Jesus. I'm pretty sure of that.'

'Yeah, true. But it is a nasty wound. He should be taken to a hospital.'

Unable to drive, Kate calls her husband who works nearby. We drive around in Mr W.'s car. I think his name is Ian, but I need to confirm that. Mr W. is very impressive as a man. He is confident, and the steering wheel makes a smooth, sensual noise when he lets it slip back into the straight-ahead position after turning a corner.

We scan the streets for Manuel. Neither of us speaks for a while, but when we do, it is initiated by Kate W.

She says, 'I can't see him.'

She says, 'This is no good, try down there. Down Green Swan Lane.'

My role is to say, 'Yes, that looks like a good place to try. There's certainly no sign of him here. Maybe Green Swan Lane is the next logical place.'

Then Kate W. nods, looking away from me. She seems very relaxed. She doesn't call her husband by his name.

'I'm glad it's you,' Kate W. says, after getting nowhere in Green Swan Lane.

'Thanks Kate. That means a lot.'

Her husband drives on through the night. Studiously scanning the glittering streets. It is he who, quite suddenly, and manfully, declares: 'He's there.'

Kate W. confirms. 'That's him.'

I agree too. Manuel is there, slumped on the pavement.

Manuel is in a bad way when we find him. His skin has greyed at the neck. He is no longer ice cold, but more like a kind of dead cold. He is just the temperature of the night air. I am amazed he is even alive, but he is. A stream of nonsensical statements comes out of his loose mouth.

'Tritty is evil,' he keeps saying as we carry him.

'Get him into this building,' Kate W. says.

It is amazing how Kate W. is still in control of this

situation, even though we are well outside the context of the SaaS startup that she founded.

We carry Manuel into a tall building.

In the building, Kate W.'s husband opens a seemingly random door. 'This way,' he says. He is much shorter than I was expecting.

'This way this way,' he says.

We are inside a flat. We follow a narrow, gleaming corridor that opens out into a large, industrial style kitchen. There is exposed brick above the double hob. Copper pans hang in bunches from steel beams.

'Get him on the table,' says Kate W.'s husband. Although he doesn't actually speak, I just know that he has spoken these words.

'It is a bad wound,' Kate W. says. 'It will need to be filled with wadding.'

I cannot speak clearly in order to agree with Kate W.

I am coping with the realisation that Kate W.'s husband is actually Tritty.

'The soft man can also be wadding,' Tritty/Kate W.'s husband says.

'I am not wadding,' I say.

'Temporarily, yes, you are wadding. If you are not wadding, then Manuel will be lost. The hole in Manuel's side cannot be healed with tape or lace or thread like a normal human wound. It must be wadded.'

Tritty takes my hand, he pinches the skin of my hand. He tugs at my skin.

'I feel uncomfortable,' I say to Kate W. Even though we are no longer in a work context, I want to make it known that this situation makes me feel very uncomfortable.

Tritty continues to tug at the skin on my hand, digging

into my flesh, cutting. But I do not bleed. Instead, my hand, my flesh and my bones become fibrous, like frayed wool.

Tritty continues to tug at me until my whole body is frayed. I become entirely made from a dense wadding material.

Tritty slowly feeds me into the wound in Manuel's side.

They tell me, the whole time, that it will only be for an interim period until Manuel is able to heal himself.

Tritty intimates to me that the former clouds have become the wine of glory and happiness.

When the wadding process is complete, I feel no pain. I feel the goodness in Manuel's slowly-healing body.

Apart from my new physical state, life continues as usual.

I make contact with my family. They say they understand. My children say they do not miss me too badly. I do my best to heal Manuel more quickly. His input is needed in the office. We miss his qualities of thoroughness, and his seemingly depthless product knowledge.

I am wadding. The office is better. I absorb the liquids produced by Manuel's wound.

I am removed from the wound after six weeks. There is a general agreement that I should be given a more senior role, at least in name, if not in remuneration. My peers respect me in a new way. They call Manuel the Egg Man and they call me the Wadding.

HOW THEY LOVED HIM

Poor Old Jonathan, that's what I say.

Just imagine – with his hands all sweaty on the steering wheel! And him swearing away.

You know how he swears in that car, don't you? P'raps with you, he tried to reign it in, when you were younger maybe. But over time, the mind slips. We're old now! You see? You don't know what we're like really, I suppose, because you were just a child.

Or maybe you do know that your lovely soft old uncle Jonno swears. You do in fact, because we drove you to the bus terminal that time, remember? When you wanted to leave early for some reason.

Bugger bugger bugger bugger bugger bugger like that, do you remember? Bugger bugger bugger every other second. Bastard vans, and bollocks whoever it was on the radio. Screaming at that foreign man in his yellow car.

Do you remember now?

Yes. I can tell from the way you're staring at the floor, that you remember now. You've got it now. You put a great deal of pressure on us that day.

That's why I wasn't with him when he went to Wickes, isn't it darling? That's why I won't go in the car at all if I can avoid it.

That's one of the reasons.

Anyway, listen to me! You're still in your coat.

Oh, it's not a coat?

How interesting the things you wear now. You've always worn these things, I suppose. Remember when you came to Sylvia's wedding and you looked like you had been clearing out the garage! You and your mother, both of you! I'm not being mean, it's just your way. We've all accepted it. That's how you are on your side.

Are you sure you're comfortable there? It's the worst possible chair you could have chosen. You're right next to **The Hole**.

You can always move if you want to. I wouldn't want to be that close to **The Hole**. We think it can 'suck in'. It has an inward sucking motion, look, even though it's completely pitch dark, you can sense a puckering, can't you? I can.

That's right, eat some cake. I'm going to join you. Fat Watchers can go hang! Oh, here's the plate so you don't get any on your house coat. Have another glass of sherry! If I can have more sherry you can have more sherry. That's the prerogative I have now. Careful of your tracksuit trousers!

Oh, I'm just joking about your clothes. I know it's not a house coat. Yes, long cardigan. Lovely material. Is it latex? Do I mean latex? I think I mean... what do I mean, Jonno?

Look at your uncle's face. He doesn't think latex is the

right word at all. Latex is for bondage, isn't it, love? For the gonks. Is that right? The gonk in the leather. Look how he's looking at me! You're ashamed of me now, Jonathan? Now that I lose my words, aren't you?

Jesus. Can you believe that he finds me embarrassing?

Have you ever considered what he's like when he's alone in a car park? Timid sort of dinosaur, aren't you Jonno?

He is.

So anyway, he's there in the car park at Wickes, fidgeting in the car seat with the engine idling.

And he's glancing at them – you know who I mean – the ones who just hang around, lurking at the hems of the car park. I don't want to say where they come from but, you know. They're allowed to work in this country. That's the law, isn't it? They're allowed. But really? Are they? It's all a bit of a grey area if you ask me. Anyway. No politics – we promised!

So he's there, aren't you dear? And he was thinking, 'Which one do I get first?'

I know this because he sent me a bloody text. *Which one do I get first?* it says.

I said, *Get the trolley first, of course. Once you've got the trolley, they know you want something else.* So he went and got a trolley. It was, you know, one of those big ones, big bit of wood on wheels really, and Jonathan gave them all the wink.

Alright – ha! Not a wink. But, you know, a nod.

About thirty seconds later, I got another text. *What now?* it said. Then another one came: *Should I get one now?*

No of course not now! They're not allowed in the shop! You don't want to lead him round the shop! He's not a kid. That's what I texted back.

Your uncle got quite cross at this point, so I had to call

him on his mobile and actually talk him through going to Wickes and buying bloody paint and plaster. He got even more huffy – he even hung up after a while - but he got all the bits and pieces, the chipboard and plaster and the paint and what have you, and all of that. To block up **The Hole**.

You might be surprised about the chipboard, but I'm not paying to have it bricked in when I don't even know how it got there.

Anyway, he piled it all up neatly and once he had paid and was out in the car park again, one of them nodded at him.

Jonathan very unsubtly nodded back and then the man came towards him. He looked very old for a, whatever, builder? Worker? Anyway, he was old. At least as old as us, and we retired, how long ago? Ages!

'You want heeelp?' That's what he said, isn't it Jonathan? When he came up to you. Like that, he speaks. 'You want heelp?' No, more like 'hilp'. Yes, like that. 'Hilp'. Ever so gentle, his voice. Quite girlish, actually.

Jonathan nodded again, I expect in a very criminal way, and took him over to the car. 'I em Cesar,' the man said. 'I em Cesar.'

'Jonathan,' said Jonathan. Didn't you darling? And then you drove home with him in the car.

You know, when Jonno first told me about those men, it was hard to believe, but I've been there, of course, I've been back and it's the easiest thing in the world. You can just pick them up. They're not shy. You just go and get one, easy as you like. Hold your nose and go for it.

So then he was here, in the house. Hail Cesar! He didn't even want a cup of tea, did he? He just cracked on with it. 'Show mi wit you want!'

Ooh, I'm getting good at doing his voice now! 'Yis,

eazie, I do thit. No problim.'

So, anyway.

It's not racist!

I can see you thinking I'm being racist, but you should have seen him! He loved it. He's not even from anywhere like that. He could be English until he speaks.

Oh shut up! Shhh.

Anyway, we showed him **The Hole**, and asked could he fix it?

He seemed confused at first, I mean, you would, but he could tell, I think, that both of us were sick – and I mean *sick* – of talking about it. Sick of having it in the lounge with us. Sick of covering it over when the neighbours came.

'We don't know how it got there!' I told him. 'We don't know why you can see whatever that is on the other side, we just want it gone. We just want it gone *instanta*.'

'Okiy,' he said.

So, we showed him what colours we wanted for the new coat, and he just carried on. When he finished, he said, 'Inything ilse?'

And well, there were the curtains, weren't there? That buggerlugs here hadn't been able to hang. So Cesar took care of that too. He was a marvel, actually. He even went out and got his own little lunch, didn't he? And he drank his beer in the garden. Very respectful, from the corner shop. I always wondered who bought that strange beer! What's wrong with Carlsberg? That's what you get isn't it, darling?

Makes him burp though. Horrible noise.

So, anyway, the thing is, Cesar was sitting out there and drinking his beer, and that was when I first noticed how your uncle Jonathan was looking at him. It wasn't all that astonishing really, looking back. But at the time, I was shocked actually. Momentarily shocked. Between us, I was quite *issed *ff actually.

Cesar - unless you see him, you wouldn't understand. Of course, you can't see him. Not now. He's basically a sort of fat Polish bloke or Croat or whatever. But he had these shy green eyes. He looked away from you, didn't he Jonathan? Go on, you can admit it. He looked away when you looked at him. Downwards, you said. Even I have to admit, he had very long eyelashes, like a horse or a pony or something. Yes, when Cesar looked away it made you feel very peaceful, you said, didn't you, Jonno? You did!

Anyway. So, it was then, really, that I understood.

It was no great astonishment when Jonathan went back to Wickes the next morning. Just stared at him, didn't you love? Just sat and stared.

Across the car park – no don't interrupt me, this is a frank family discussion. We have nothing to hide. We can tell family anything. Anyway, it became heart breaking. Darling Jonathan. To think of him there, just longing to see those askance green eyes, those horsey lashes.

I realised that if he was going to have what he wanted, then it would be better if it was someone like Cesar because, well, he's basically nobody. Who knows him?

So, I said, just go back. Go on go back and have a word with him. Didn't I? Go and see if he's, you know, available for more work. We've got plenty he can be getting on with.

Well, I was, if I'm being very honest, it was painful. It was painful. It took me a few glasses of wine, and a couple of Mum's old jellies to get the nerve up, but I suppose, what does it matter? I have to be honest, after I'd given myself those new shoes this year.

And Jonno never gets anything for himself.

There had been his little friend, Clive. I remember, when I first met Jonno. Little chubby Clive, but he sort of moved on when I came onto the scene. It was sad really. Everyone loved Clive.

Anyway – the point is, Jonno should get something, that's what I thought.

And Cesar wasn't exactly expensive, was he? For plastering and such, at least, he was very reasonable. So, once it was decided, it was like everything else: I took charge of course. I had to dress him up, poor Jonno. I had to give him the right shirt and his best jacket – you know the cream coloured one? He looks about a thousand years old in that stiff wax coat he's normally tramping about in. So, I spruced him up, best I could, and we went to the car park together.

There were dozens of them, a hundred maybe. All men. All with the same look in their eye and not at all clean. You know, I used to – in the day – I used to enjoy that. A bit of rough we called it. There were a lot to choose from. Much younger, much taller and with swarthy, you know, looks. But Jonathan had been bitten, by something. It could only be Cesar. He was really pining for that chubby little old man.

I saw him after a few minutes and walked straight over to him, with Jonno, old buggerlugs, shuffling after me. Sort of wheezing I suppose you'd call it, or panting.

'Really, at our age, it's stupid to get so worked up about it,' I said. Anyway, it was clear that Jonathan wasn't going to follow the thing through, so it was me, wasn't it? I went right up to Cesar.

'Cesar,' I said. 'No it's not about your work. It was excellent. I mean, **The Hole** is still giving us sleepless nights, and is quite large now, but we can hardly blame you for that,' I reassured him. 'Those curtains really are marvellously hung. No, no, let me finish, Cesar, please. We just wanted to say thank you, properly. For everything you did. Won't you come to our house for dinner tonight?'

'I wirk?' he said.

'No no no – just come round,' I told him. 'Silly Cesar. We'll cook a nice meal. I do Chinese or curry on Thursdays. I get special packs. Come to same address as before?'

'I no no,' he said. You know how they look sort of scared of you? God. It was like coaxing a bird or something.

'Don't be rude, Cesar!' I said. 'Come on, it'll be nice. Jonno will pick you up again? Yes? Six o'clock. Yes? Dinner. Beer. Yes?'

'Oki. Oki.'

And so it was all arranged. Oki Oki.

Predictably, Jonno became very bold in Sainsbury's, didn't you? Honestly! He was actually strutting in the crisp aisle, proudly brandishing a bag of kettle crisps at me. I tried to tell him that Cesar wouldn't want kettle crisps, they're not interested in mesquite and sweet chilli!

But he was adamant. Really forceful actually. We got a few cans of the beer Cesar likes – Sainsbury's has a shelf just for that stuff now. You know, special pickles and gherkins and all sorts. That's the way it is now, you know? Fine by me, I suppose. As long as they pay the tax, what can you do?

So. I cooked a curry beef stew, which is like curry, but it's my mild version. I'll give you the recipe. I buy in popp-a-doms usually, but we already had the kettle crisps, so we had those. We had Dubonnet, obviously, for in the living room.

Anyway, long story short – we went all out. Clever Jonathan had the idea to pick up Cesar in the Jag. Such a treat for him. They probably dream of owning even a normal car, like a Passat or something. So he thought the Jag would set the right tone.

And I got the house all nice and put things out we might want later.

It took a long time for you to come back, though darling, didn't it? I remember. An age! And I was thinking to myself, they've eloped! They've skulked off to a – oh I don't know, an alley or something. But it was just a mix up, Cesar had ended up working on a house right on the other side of the next village down.

Not to be deterred, Jonathan stayed in the car park and just waited.

And waited.

Eventually, he started driving around, looking for signs of Cesar. I believe he got quite panicky actually. You hear stories about people, even grown men, just disappearing. Imagine how bad his anxiety gets when he loses his immigrant worker! Bugger bugger bugger bollocks. Oh, his poor heart! Your poor heart!

Anyway, eventually, Jonathan found him in that café they all go to, and stood in the doorway until Cesar came over. There was some kind of misunderstanding or something, Jonathan didn't really tell me what, and I won't bore you with it, but eventually – at last! – they got home and we all tucked into the beefy stew curry.

Cesar was wearing, I have to assume it was his best pullover. He and Jonathan hardly looked at each other the whole time while we ate. We said about how good the curtains were a few times. We examined **The Hole**, and then covered it with a rag.

We drank, and I'll be honest, I added a little bit of

something extra into the beer. Something from the chemist I get to help me sleep, if you know what I mean, just to help Cesar relax a bit.

Cesar ate precisely zero kettle crisps, as predicted.

Well, it wasn't long before we were all three sheets, weren't we? And I had been topping us up – naughty me! – with Mum's jellies.

When I suggested we play strip poker, there was absolutely no resistance. It was that easy. I remember thinking, we're just animals really, and so why not! Why bloody not.

I'm going to tell you the whole story, alright, so we're not blood related, are we? You call him uncle Jonno, but you're virtually a stranger. Don't look so shocked. You're not going anywhere. Cesar was especially beautiful naked. He had the smoothest back I've ever seen on a man. Like baby skin it was. And he had a very dusky bottom. He did, a dusky bottom and great big balls with soft hair all over them. He was quite drunk, and shy looking. Being honest, he was bloody dreadful at poker. So am I, as you probably know – awful! So, it was me in my bra, and Cesar in nothing at all, and Jonathan sort of glowering at us both. In his vest and trousers. You could see he was very excited.

So, I didn't bother waiting for Jonathan, I just put my hand over on Cesar's thigh and started stroking it. He got this long smooth erection, very quickly. It was really long but not very wide, like a kind of whistle. Very noble actually. I stroked it for a while, and then leant over and popped it in my mouth. Very strong tasting, it was. Hard work will do that to a glans. And, as we know, he drank no water, just beer. I don't mind really. I like to eat kidneys right up to the sell-by date. I don't mind strong meat.

So, I was doing my thing, wondering if Jonno was ever

going to get up the nerve to join in. I could hear him behind me, panting and sort of laboriously getting out of his slacks whilst sitting in the dining chair. Then I heard his chair crash to the ground and felt him creaking up behind me. Sort of looming over us.

Cesar went rigid then. 'No him, no him,' he started saying and he pushed himself backwards. Gently pushing my head away.

'But Cesar, darling,' I said. But he was backing away and looking, I mean why do they look so bloody terrified of us? It makes you feel like a monster. Don't even try mentioning money.

Anyway, we sort of negotiated something and I went back to what I was doing. It seemed to appease him. But still, every time Jonathan came near us, Cesar tried to scrabble away. He was too drunk to stand though, and he fell on the floor, didn't he darling? A couple of times.

Anyway, something must have kicked in, because Cesar eventually gave in to the idea. He became much more pliable with a few more sprinkles of my pills.

It became clear that Jonahthan couldn't control himself any longer. It was all actually very exciting, even though, I had resigned myself to the fact that nobody was going to do anything for me at this stage. We had gone beyond the things that I find pleasurable.

I left them to it if you must know. I've always found Jonathan's tongue a bit embarrassing, in the intimate sense, and it was everywhere on Cesar. Uncontrolled – Labradorian!

As I left the room, it was getting very thrashy and boyish. Really, a lot of thrashing. And the noise! But there's only so much you can struggle, isn't there?

I went to bed in the end. Sounds ridiculous, doesn't it? But you have to remember, these were both quite old men, so it was all going to either crescendo quickly, or die a death.

It can't have taken that long because after a bit more bashing about it went quiet. I remember thinking, have we made a mistake? But it was only fleetingly. Too late anyway.

Jonathan hasn't – you know – lost control for a long time. He hasn't done his thing, not for decades, and even then, it was just something he needed to try out, if it went too far, then it was just youth. Just youth, eh, Jonno?

Look at him! A different species, I swear to God. He doesn't like it when I do the hands. I'm just doing the gesture now, Jonno, this strangulation gesture you don't like!

You know what I'm saying. You get the picture. Big hands. Clumsy bloody grip. You must remember when you were first in love, and there was a bit of you know. A little bit of throttling now and again. A little *grrrrr round the nnneck.*

Well, it's been donkey's years for us, since Jonno lost control. So, I don't think I should have worried really. Couldn't have been predicted.

Anyway, I couldn't physically do anything to stop it going wrong, so I fell asleep.

I came down the next morning, to find things pretty much – *as expected* – worst case scenario. You can still see signs, if you look closely.

Jonno's been very sheepish about where Cesar is now.

But, as you can see, *that thing, that gaping hole is back again!* There is a wind from it now, and a soft sort of foreign voice. *Where is the wind coming from?* I don't even think it's in the same place as before. How can it move around like that?

You really shouldn't sit so close to it. We were going to call the council, but they won't come.

I think it's even grown since you arrived. I'd get away from the area, please, if you don't mind. Sit somewhere else. Use your sense! Not there!

That's it. That's better. I think you excited it then.

I mean, what are we meant to do about that?

LOW ENERGY MEETING

Transcript begins:
The team are gathering in Room A. The Line Manager is
already there. He stands, talking and gesticulating. He seems
highly stimulated. You cannot see the entire room due to the
restricted camera, but you should know that there is one main
entrance to the board room, Room A, and then a smaller door
which leads to a technical area, which we will now refer to as
Room B. The door to Room B is closed.

Thanks for coming. So many of you! Come in, come
in, that's OK. I brought treats because we've all got low
energy. You don't have to eat them. It's a treat, that's all.
Maltesers, I know, but it's OK. I'm already beyond help.

Is Sabrina coming? My God, Sabrina, you look so well.
All the teeth have grown back? Wonderful. Good.

So. Oh – here come some late ones. Come in, come in.

It's alright. I've had too much coffee, Sharon. That's why I'm talking so much while you're clearly trying to find a seat. Have you succeeded? Well done. These chairs are so impractical aren't they? Cost the earth, did you know that? Anyway. Some people love them.

Alright, everyone safe? Good, you seem safe. Things I hear have been going strangely on the second and third floors. A slime leak, is that right? I'm hearing a slime leak has taken place. Simon, we can have your take on that later please.

I have my own update to give, just quickly, before we begin, on the purging of Building Two. Most of you know that Sam, Raj, Anna and a few others took on the task of purging Building Two, after it became the target of a focus beam, we think, from one of the new mountains.

Well, you also probably know that Raj gained an eye during the first approach. A third eye, that's right, on his neck. He says he cannot use it at all, but he has accepted that surgery will probably make it worse. He has also agreed to switch roles so that the eye cannot accidentally see any sensitive material.

Building Two is now officially condemned, as far as we are concerned. So, that's good news, although we are going to allow it remain standing in case we anger the, er, I don't know what they are called really. Beings? Whatever they are. I think of them as beings, but I am told *gathered energy* is what some people are thinking. Anyway, they have that building and we can't really do anything about it.

Oh – more at the door? So, come in, come in!

We need to get started, if possible. One more Malteser. Yes! Delicious. One swig of water, quite a sticky mouth!

Alright. So, bit different today, but I'm going to talk to

you all about when I was at school. Normally, yes, exactly Mike, normally I take questions whenever you want, but I need to get through this story please, it won't seem to make sense, then it will, then it possibly won't and then at the end, well, who knows. Maybe this time, it will turn out, that we have finally solved all our problems.

Maybe we will be able to rest at last. Eh? Some rest. Imagine, a weekend!

Anyway.

[Transcriber's note] The Line Manager pauses. He sways – it is barely perceptible on screen, but with freeze-framing it is clear to see him sway a little. He looks towards the door that leads to Room B. Then he takes another Malteser and seems to swallow it whole. When he speaks next, he speaks quickly, without giving himself space to really engage the colleagues in the room. Many of the attendees do not catch up with what he's saying until he is a good way into his description of falling in love.

As I was saying, I'd like to bring to your attention a story from my childhood. Alright? I was a child, as you can imagine, with some difficulties mixing with people. You know I am a quiet man. I won't lie. My leadership style is low-volume. Yes?

I was bullied, is the truth. Quite systematically. By that I mean it was a total form of being bullied. The face and the voice and the actions of my bully were with me at all times. His prowess on the football pitch was with me when I stood in my little back yard holding a stick and hitting the fence with it. His voice was there in the toilet when I could not control my stream. In the dark, his lean shape and his onion head we propped outside my window, making the calling sounds of the night.

Max – the boy's name was Max - was everywhere. I was obsessed with him in two ways. Firstly, I was obsessed with his existence – the faint smell of rugs and smoke that came from his clothes, his voice that sounded pinched off, as though he wasn't allowed to raise his voice – like he had trained himself to cut you with his voice rather than to shout at you. Secondly, the practical obsession, in which I spent hour after dreadful hour, wondering what Max would do to me. Would it be nothing? Would it be violence? Would it be silence?

The silences were worst. Silences in which he led all the other kids, in which I was left to drown as they looked through me, vanished me, though I shook and trembled and begged them to stop.

It was after a full, exhausting week of such silence that I fell in love with him. Something seemed to break in me during that silent week. It let me look at Max and, since he had to pretend I didn't exist, I began staring at him. At his neck, at the mole on his collarbone. At his wrists and his v-shaped body. I spent the week in school staring at his body, listening to his snide remarks – sometimes about me but, often, intentionally about someone else. Something that would prove he was ignoring me. At home, I drew him. I sat up in bed and drew him endlessly. In every picture, Max was covered in wounds and all smashed up, needing to be rescued. I thought I was punishing him, but the wounded Max I drew was captured so tenderly, it seems inconceivable to me now that I didn't notice I was falling in love with him.

When it hit – the final culmination of my week of devoted, sickened drawing and staring – the force of my love was overwhelmingly powerful. I loved him as entirely, as consumingly as I had feared him. More. I loved him like I was exploding, like I was boiling in adrenaline. It lasted only a fraction of a moment, but it was a sun-like feeling, a radiance that seemed to dissolve my actual flesh.

I do not want to remind people of flesh dissolving, especially after some of the reports we had last month in the Basingstoke office, but this was a metaphorical dissolution. His hold over me was so strong, I melted away. I had lived with this shameful need for his approval for so long, that when it turned into love, it surged out of me. It bulged and swelled and emerged out of me. And I mean literally – it emerged out of me. Like – out of my mouth, in a physical shape.

I'm looking around the room and sensing that you were not expecting me to talk about this. It's not the usual message, for a strategy meeting. Especially when we have all of this – I'm looking for a word now – I am thinking of 'chaos'? Yes? We have all of this chaos. Right outside the window. In this very building!

We've got slime leaks. We've got those recent mountains. We've got some other things we have not touched on today, and which I know many of you are still recovering from physically and emotionally.

I would also include in this 'chaos' the really innovative ways some of you have been approaching your tasks. I've seen some approaches that have really dazzled me. But also alarmed me.

They have alarmed us all.

So, as I say, there is a lot happening, but I promise, there is a reason for me to be talking about this massive physically-manifested love I felt for Max when we were

alone in the classroom and he finally, after a week of
shunning me and leading a general shunning against me
with the rest of the class, finally said, 'Alright,' to me. He
said, 'Alright,' meaning good morning. Meaning, 'You are
given life again. I allow it.'

I was overwhelmed. 'Alright,' I said. The words barely came
out. My lips were like felt, and had no purchase on my words.
'How are you?' I asked. 'I saw the match at the weekend.'

'What?'

'My mum and some friends took me to see the Villa
game. It was amazing!'

He leapt at me, put his hands around my throat and
shoved me backwards. 'Shut the fuck up!' he said.

I might have a quick Malteaser now.

I went rigid. He grabbed me again, this time around the
collar. He said to me, 'I don't give a shit about your mum,
or her friends.'

My whole body was limp, I could not raise so much as a
finger to defend myself. Max put his face so close to me, I
could feel his hot breath going into me –his hot ginger-bis-
cuit air. That was the moment, with his hands choking me,
with his lips millimetres from my own, that was when it
hit – the surge.

All I could see was him. The broad white expanse of his
moonish head – it was like I was standing on the surface
of him, his head was the whole world, a vast lonely desert.
I explored the landscape of him. His translucent blue eyes,
and his shocked small mouth.

Is everyone following this?

I know, it sounds like a sort of Stockholm thing, doesn't
it, Sharon? I personally think it was more complex than
simple Stockholm syndrome, but you could be right about

that, actually. It hardly matters. What matters is that I was pre-teen, and getting confused by absolutely everything. I manifested the perfect conditions for this powerful surge of love. A love so swollen and sudden and poisoned that I could feel it rising up, out of me. I thought it was just going to be vomit, so I shoved Max away.

'I'm going to puke!' I said. 'I need to get to the toilet.'

'Puke here,' he said. 'Puke in this room.'

And he was going to watch me puke, but then the bell rang. People were starting to come in. I took advantage of this moment of distraction and rushed to the toilet, clutching my hand to my lips, pressing back at whatever was about to spew out.

I just made it to the toilet. Unable to hold back any more, I lowered my hands, and let my love come out of me.

It emerged from me in the shape of a human man, in a dressing gown, with thinning hair, and an oven glove on one hand. This man was crying inconsolably.

He walked towards the mirror, where he rubbed his grey hair with his oven glove, and stared into the mirror and wept.

I held out a hand, obviously I didn't touch him. I couldn't touch him,. But I held out a hand, as a gesture. The gesture spooked my love greatly. He wiped his eyes on the dressing gown sleeve, and bolted.

I wanted to follow my love, to catch up with him and see what his deal was. I shouted, 'Where are you going?' but he did not respond. The next thing that happened was my teacher came into the toilets to see if I was alright, and I had to go back to the classroom. I worried about it all that afternoon – what would happen if my love was seen, wondering around, blubbing? In a school too! I knew enough to realise that would be awkward at the very least.

What if my love was arrested as some kind of pervert?

I tried to find him at break, and then again at lunch, but it was no use. He had gone. Only the ache in my jaw told me he had even existed at all. I went home, I ate dinner, I watched television, I talked to my mum about nothing. I did everything as I normally did. For a few hours, I looked out of the window to see if he was there. My crying old man love in the street beyond our back garden. He was not there. Armed with a tennis racket, I went to see if he was in my sister's room, but he was not.

He was nowhere. He was gone. Until he came back.

Now, I'm looking around the room and I see some of you get it now. My love, the old man, returned just a few months ago. Not just to me, but to almost all of us. I know we have been here before. We were all convinced – *convinced* – that we had discovered the root cause of all this when we ousted the moth infestation from Mike's house. Those moths had been proven, we thought, to be the root cause of everything. The mountains, the slime leak, the tear in the fabric of reality, all could be explained back to the movement of the moth wings in Mike's garage.

And we burnt Mike's house down for nothing. We got it wrong. So I am being cautious now. But. But – well, let me continue, and then we will see if you agree with me. If maybe this is a thread we can follow.

Yes, my love came back. I found him downstairs in my kitchen, weeping uncontrollably at the dinner table. Luke, the man who lodges in my spare bedroom, said he didn't know whether to call the police.

'Has he said anything?' I asked. 'Has he mentioned me?'

'He just sits there. I've tried making him breakfast,' Luke told me, 'but he's not having it.'

We watched my love crying for a full hour. All the while, Luke was desperate to get rid of him, getting more and more agitated. He became quite rude actually, especially considering he was a lodger who pays almost nothing towards household expenses, and has transformed my daughter's old bedroom to such an extent that I can't seriously expect her to ever stay there again.

Anyway, I did eventually call the police, just to silence Luke and his babbling. They came and took my love away in their car. Something about having to touch the physical shape of my love made the police officers feel very uncomfortable. It was similar to the way Andrew Gallery reacts if he hasn't had his lunch and you ask him a difficult question.

Yes, Andrew, we all know about that, and I want you to know, we understand, and I will always have snacks.

The police became short tempered, is what I'm saying. Hangry, some people call it. The police seemed hangry as soon as they had to touch my love with their hands. They became surly with me, especially the older of the two officers. His name was Braine and he gave me a savage look as they got ready to drive the old, male manifestation of my love away.

'This is not why I joined the police,' he seemed to be saying with his craggy police-y face.

Anyway, it didn't make any difference having my love arrested. He was released with no charge and came back almost within the month, crying again and bothering Luke so much that he eventually moved out. Then he began to appear to other people. He startled my mother by manifesting himself under the mahogany breakfast bar. He followed my poor son down a hill.

He says nothing, he only cries. He cries and cries. Now, I know that some of you are starting to make connections, because of course, my love has appeared to you also.

There is a lull in the proceedings. The Line Manager sits for a while. Everyone else keeps their eyes to themselves. Nobody wants to look. The Line Manager, after a period of stillness, glances up at the security camera. He seems to be looking at us, although he cannot know that we would recover this footage, or that we would be watching all of this play out. He takes a breath and, apparently at random, puts his arm on the shoulder of a colleague. The colleague is Sharon.

Oh Sharon, you look exhausted. I know this has affected you in particular. Please, please have chocolate, have one, have one. You all must have one and then please let's crack on. We have to crack on.

So, Sharon, at some point in this meeting we should hear from you, about your hotel that you built. Don't look at your feet, Sharon. We are all interested in your recent establishment of a boutique hotel on the eighth floor of this building. Your hotel has, I believe, added nine more floors to the building. All structurally sound, I'm told, although of course, when we get to the bottom of what is actually happening, it will probably have to be torn down. In fact, this whole business park will probably have to be torn down, or abandoned at the very least.

It is a tasteful hotel, Sharon. You have a great deal to be proud of. I heard that some of the Customer Care team were a bit upset because you took their area. I don't know that they are happy, actually, to work in the lobby of your hotel. Even if they do benefit from discounted use of the spa and beauty centre. However, I feel sure they will come to realise it is a very tasteful hotel.

I have stayed in the hotel, actually Sharon, and I found the experience a real delight. I booked in just for a couple of nights, just to see how it was. I found the waiting staff especially cordial.

I met the ambassador in the bar on my first night. He was just where you said he would be, in the specially delegated diplomatic booth. He was surrounded by paperwork and drinking a hot martini, which is a new craze, I hear.

We talked about the trouble the Ambassador has been having in explaining to the people back home what has been going on here, and what can be done to navigate our way out of the situation. He told me that his masters back home had not asked him why he was staying in your hotel and not, for example, in the ambassadorial residence they keep in rural Oxfordshire, or the city pied-à-terre that is part of his remuneration package.

He asked me to show him a data slime lake, which I was happy to do. We examined a sample of the data slime, although it was not possible to know what data we were looking at. I explained to the ambassador that the measure of slime we fished out could contain anything. It might have contained all the names and addresses of all the salon owners that have ever been registered in the North East of England. Or it could just as easily have been barn measurements. The ambassador seemed very happy with the idea it might have been barn measurements. The dimensions of various barns, he said, made him think of his childhood, on the large farm his parents owned, where he would spend a lot of time looking at their barn. Maybe – and I'm filling in the blanks a bit here – he remembered touching the wooden doors and exploring the old fibres of the timber and smelling the soil and wind and insect life that was abundant on that farm that his parents owned.

After our excursion to the slime lake, we returned to the hotel, and the ambassador listened sympathetically to our predicament. With the slime. With the beings. Et cetera. I did not allude specifically to the problem of the physical human shape of my love; it seemed like small potatoes. But I can say that, in general, he understands, I think, better than we might have expected. At the conclusion of our evening meal, I recall, he spread his broad hands and, in a shrug, he said, 'We all are slaves to democracy.'

The following morning, I came down to breakfast in the lobby, hoping to see the ambassador and talk more to him, but instead, there was only my love, weeping as usual.

I decided to try a loftier approach with my love. The Ambassador's charisma had been somewhat infectious, and I felt quite primed and on good form. He had treated me as an equal, after all. He had laughed at several of my jokes about the contents of the slime lake, and even some of the darker jibes about the intentions of the Beings who now occupy a substantial area of the business park.

I reminded myself that I had been very successful in my Leadership and Inspiration modules. I have a few tricks up my sleeve.

With some patience, and wielding a breakfast hot martini, I managed to coax my love out of his stupor, and into talking to me.

I asked him how he'd been. My love told me that he had managed to stop crying for a short time, but had taken it up again because he could not stop thinking about a tragic space shuttle accident that took place in the 1980s. His mind had been plagued with it, he said, as though someone had injected the disaster into his spinal fluid, is how he put it. Someone – or something – had placed it inside him and he could not make it go away.

He told me he could only see the astronauts in the cockpit of the shuttle as children. He saw them die in fear and panic, but also in a combustion of their dreams, and the dreams of all children, which he now laments, he told me, every time he smells petrol. He cried, he told me, as though it had been my death. Or the deaths of my brother and sister. As though he had seen me die.

I lost patience because at this point he started blubbing again and spilt most of his hot martini right in the eyeline of the ambassador, which was very embarrassing.

I asked him if his sadness was really so much that it prevented him from getting dressed. But he simply went on about the shuttle accident, as though I hadn't even spoken.

He told me that he sees everyone I know dying in that shuttle cockpit. He told me, everyone I know is burning in a cockpit, and that is why he was wearing that terrible dressing gown.

The Line Manager sips his coffee and, with freeze frame and zoom, we see that he takes a moment to reflect on the idea of everyone he knows dying in a shuttle accident .

Sharon, I'll give your hotel an excellent rating on TripAdvisor.

Because, and this is my real point – everyone, Sharon, I know that you have all had to creep around this particular issue, with me especially, and I don't want anyone imagining that they have to walk on eggshells – but...

It was him, wasn't it? Who asked you to build the hotel.

My love, somehow materialising and crying at the breakfast table in your one bedroom flat, Sharon, inspired you to build a hotel that defies all known engineering, right here on top of our head office. Not only that – it was him who inspired you to invite the ambassador who uses it as his second residence and has advanced the stature of our company beyond measure.

So, I can see there is agitation in the room. Can I have a show of hands from anyone who has been visited in their kitchen or another communal area of their home or public space by an old man in a rank dressing gown, wearing an oven glove on one hand, and crying uncontrollably? Think carefully. Really try to remember. I can see several hands going up in the air. Good. Communication then, mmm? We have not communicated this to each other as well as we could have done. I could have been more forthcoming about the time I blurted a fully-grown man – whole – from my mouth at the age of about twelve. And you could all have been clearer that a man who meets this description has been appearing in your homes and in your lives.

In the interests of disclosure to the full group – some of you have come forward to tell me about this apparition. So, to you, I have only been filling in the detail. Would any of you like to describe the first day you came into your kitchen and found the physical manifestation of my love for my childhood bully sitting there crying?

Yes. Michelle, please do contribute. You found him there in December, I remember you saying. Yes, that was it. Your mother was expecting to find Peter, her friend. Peter, who was going to look at her car for her, wasn't he? It had been making that noise. But there wasn't Peter, there was my love, in fits of despair. He smashed over the box of Cheerios, if I remember your recollection correctly. It was a harrowing experience, wasn't it? With toddlers in the house. But then, he inspired you to rub special salt into your back, and now you have grown wings.

Polly, can you tell us your experience? For the benefit of those who are conferencing in from Harlow and can't see, Polly says she had returned from leading a neighbourhood ant-kill to find my love in her kitchen scrooching and raging with his head in the larder. Polly still had on her protective clothing, and was still covered in sputum, and holding the six-foot mandible from the massive ant she had killed, and was looking forward to something to eat, but my love made it absolutely impossible. But it was him, wasn't it?

Everyone, it was my love, sitting in the kitchen, who inspired Polly to rise up and lead her community in the fight against the giant ants.

I understand, it's difficult, but we need to get this out in the open. My love, in the form of a frail and slightly transparent old man, weeping about things like the deaths of two astronauts in a tragedy that happened decades ago, is blind sentimentality and it is causing real problems to our productivity.

I know several of you have told me that you like it, and you don't want the appearances to stop. You tell me the apparitions have solved huge problems in your life. You have risen above what you were before.

You send me flowers, which I should say now is welcome, but very wasteful. If you must express your gratitude, I suggest a donation to charity. Or a quiet nod as we pass each other around the office.

The line manager seems to go through a physical gear change. While the rest of the participants in the meeting are visibly flagging, perhaps due to fumes emitted by what we now know was a severe type six slime leak, the Line Manager rubs his face and shakes his arms, much like someone in front of a mirror, psyching themselves up for a difficult encounter, like a job interview or lunch with someone you are divorcing. After a few moments of reflection and silence, he turns to the subject of dealing with the apparition of his love.

I mentioned to you earlier that I saw my love in one of the magnificent spaces in the hotel that Sharon constructed. I mentioned that he told me a story about astronauts making him sad. I did not tell you that I then followed him, my old love, through the lobby to the lift.

I stood in the lift with him, hardly breathing. As you know, if you do not interact with the physical manifestation of my love, he does not acknowledge that you are there. He perceives no threat.

So he did not stop me when, on arriving at his floor, I followed him to his room. Before he could close the door, I followed him inside. Inside the room, he behaved in much the same way he always has, he sat in his grotty dressing gown and sniffled and bloored.

He barely resisted – barely resisted at all – when I shoved him onto the bed, and rolled him up in the duvet. I felt him, like a dog in a sleeping bag, the muscles of him, but also the uselessness of his movements. He did not know how to escape the rolled-up duvet. I wrapped him further in the double sheet, and then used the ties from two of the magnificent robes that Sharon, to your credit, you have hanging in every room of the hotel. I tied each end like a long, weeping boiled sweet.

I won't tell you which of Sharon's staff I paid to help me load him into a laundry bin and wheel him to the lift.

He barely resisted, is the main point. He is not even really a human, after all. He emerged, as I said, painfully through my mouth just as I felt the strange surge of love for the boy who was, at that moment, insulting my mother. He emerged as the physical presence of loving someone from whom you cannot protect the people you love. The love that emerges when you are faced with the blank face of hatred.

Which is to say, it might well resemble a man, but it is not a man. I have trussed him. From what I can see, he does not bruise.

You might remember that at the beginning of this transcription, Door B was highlighted. As he says the words 'does not bruise', the Line Manager rises from his chair and produces a key fob from his pocket. He opens Door B. A strange light comes from inside the room.

Do not be alarmed, everyone. We will simply go in as a group. This love of mine came out whole, and must go back in whole. I've spoken to my own line manager, and we have agreed that the best course of action is for you to help me by feeding my love back into my mouth.

Some of you will need to hold open my mouth. I think at least four of you for that task. The rest of you will feed him into me.

We must hope that he will soften, yes. Much depends on him softening or all will be lost.

THE SIEGE

*Enter **Host**.*

So, there you are again. Ah. It is you, isn't it? Let
me inspect you. Yes, I lost my glasses. I had a spare
pair, you know? Ace & Tate – do you remember?
Excellent value. Excellent design.

*The Host peers closely at us, his invited audience. He looks
at us, and beyond us. Focusing on our shape, and then on
somewhere in the darkening area behind us.*

Yes. Yes, I see. I can confirm – you are you. Welcome. Welcome all of you. Late though. I suppose
you have considered that. Must be a reason for it.
Out of your hands, eh? Never mind. I am prepared.
As you can see, I have dressed.

Our Host raises his arms in the air, his hands poised as if they are moving to chamber music. He is presenting himself to us. He is displaying his comportment, like a dancer in a music box. He seems to want to make it clear that he is wearing multiple shirts, the kind that once would have been work clothes, suitable for a relaxed office environment. The various single-colour, easy-iron garments are all made from one hundred percent cotton, but they are rags now, hanging off our Host in frayed layers. The way the Host moves in them, we suppose, is meant to seem foppish and bohemian.

I have done my best to dress well. I never used to bother with it at all, you know.

The Host gestures to the wreckage around him. His gestures, if followed, land the eye upon torn floorboards, dust pools, various empty bottles, scattered silicon spatulas.

Shall I give you a twirl?

The Host twirls around, a giddy pirouette he might call it. He trips on a dusty volume of Yotam Ottolenghi's vegetarian masterpiece, PLENTY. The trip on PLENTY sends him sprawling, he almost falls upon a member of the audience – it is a staged fall that forces the member of the audience to put out an 'arm' to stop the Host from colliding with them.

Good hands! Nice catch! Thank you, no –

The Host recoils from the 'touch' of the audience, which of course did not happen. There is never any touching of the hosts.

– don't actually put your hands on my, ah, body. Please, if you don't mind. I think some manners must still be observed, I am not here to be hauled about, you know! Scandalous!

The Host, feigning offence, draws himself back from us, like a cobra. He hisses, and then it is no longer a joke. He turns away, and then sets off on an angry little tour around the ruined kitchen, climbing over upturned mid-century dining chairs, stepping around heaps of rubble and scatter cushions. He no longer seems aware of us, but is fixated on his precise journey around the room. Each destination, and the order and manner in which he must arrive is predetermined. We get the sense that there are journeys like this in response to many of his emotions. For example, now he has been offended and so he must take a very specific path on his way to touch the author's photo of Delia Smith, and then, on his return trip, run a finger along the cratered slate work top. After a diversion that takes him to the far end of the kitchen, where there are two columns of biographical art books and spineless architecture hardbacks, he returns. By the time he gets back to us, he seems sheepish.

I apologise. You did not mean to touch me. It was my fault, utterly my fault. Besides, I must feel strange to you. Not at all good to touch.

There is a flash of rib at this moment, the Host's reduced grey skin poking out from under his many ragged shirts. The Host brazenly exposes this part of his body, then a little bit of his shoulder, before hiding it all away again. He is toying with us, we assume he supposes.

Naturally, after so much time, things have got quite bad. Quite irregular, with my exercise routine. The kettle bell is over there somewhere – completely unused. It's hard to keep any sort of tone. Of course, you'll have to, aha, excuse the mess.

There is another motion or gesture of the Host's body. Under the lifted shirts, his torso hairs are thick and rugged looking.

We, the audience are motioned deeper into the kitchen while the Host continues – like a shadow – to slither across the walls, passing his strings of arms over several empty frames, a shredded French poster detailing the anatomy of poisonous and edible mushrooms, a tin sign that says, Northern Soul, Keep the Faith. Wherever he moves, the Host gestures to some area of the kitchen and smiles, inviting us to see the ruin of it. He seems determined to show how bad things are, and yet also to show us what he still has, and we have lost.

Right inside. That's it! Come in with you! It's not dangerous. I don't think we will use any of the other rooms. You can ignore the hallway, I've utterly given up on that. And that door: pay it no mind. I don't even notice it anymore. Must look bloody terrible, unpainted et cetera.

Ah – so, this is the kitchen. As you know, we did all the work ourselves. Still went miles over budget, but who doesn't? It's funny, you go into these things, and you – you don't think it will happen to you. You don't know what to expect at all. Nobody knows what to expect, do they? That's what we kept telling ourselves. Everyone goes through this, that's what we said. Everyone goes through hell. Do you find that? Has anyone else ever mentioned anything about that to you? Can you tell me?

We do not answer the Host. We remain silent. It would be nice, some of us think, to tell him that yes, everyone has said something like this, they have all done this. But we can't, any more than we can touch him. Realising what he has said, the Host remains still and quite blanched for a time. To us, it could be 40-43 seconds. To the Host? Who knows? He has a clock somewhere, we assume, or not.

You should have seen the state of this worktop this morning – you would have asked yourself, is he collecting those flies? Does he have plans for them? And the answer is no. But I do have names for them! Ha ha! I have given them all names, it sounds like a joke, but it's true. These flies here, look, actually don't.

The Host fidgets. He has come down from some high he was on. He gropes the air towards the open copy of Dishoom 'From Bombay With Love'. He seems to want to plot a course for it, but he is stuck holding several flies that he has pulled out from somewhere under his shirts.

No, don't look at them. I'm ashamed.

The Host flings all the flies away. Their bodies bounce near the sink, and ping off the light fixtures.

It was a joke, that's all. I thought of it for a long time, telling someone that joke. I didn't know it would be you. I hoped someone else would come. Listen, try to hear how it would have sounded if someone else had come. Imagine some musicality in it:

Look at all these flies! I don't have a use for them, no. Dot dot dot – but I do have names for them all! You see? Funny. No, perhaps not. Perhaps not at all. The timing. It must be something wrong with the timing on that one. I can assure you that I used to be very funny indeed. Perhaps you know that already? Someone in here must have seen me before? You must have done. I told lots of jokes. If you could ask my friends, you would know. They would tell you that actually, I am funny, and that joke is funny. It is funny.

Look, I'm smiling, I'm laughing at my joke, you see? You – you there, I see you in the audience, your faces are becoming clearer to me now, I suppose I am getting used to the light. Yes, you over there, you smiled. I saw you.

Assuredly, none of us has smiled. Although we may have wanted to – when our faces become visible, it's natural to want to do things with them. A residue of desire to show expression, to communicate sympathetically. And this – we are told – this could be the last time we are allowed to come. But assuredly, we do not smile.

Anyway, I have wiped that whole area diligently. But somehow they keep coming – the flies keep coming. I see nothing else. Sometimes, I think I can hear something else coming in. I think I can hear the rustling of someone. Like when we first moved in, and the boy would be there, suddenly, grinning beside the fridge. Or someone would be visiting, and I would look round and see their face. Sometimes, I hear a rustling noise and I peer in the direction it came from. I try to see people, but there is nobody, of course. The sound was just my arm moving. My sockets – shoulders and hips, you know? They make such a terrible sound. Gah, I clean up as best I can. I have very limited cleaning resources because I can't access the utility room.

You know, my one regret is that we never finished the utility room to my satisfaction. You can't go and see it – nobody please go in the utility room, I beg you. I beg you, not in there. Just trust me when I say we never got around to painting it properly at all. In fact, we ran out of money completely when it came to the utility room. It was all freecycle and things we found on the pavement. We would scour the freebies. You had to be on there at the right times. Get in early and phone to make sure they knew, or text to make sure they knew someone was coming. They are on their way, and so it's a commitment now.

Yes, I was off out all over town, on the bus. All over town to collect things for the utility room. There was a family in Brixton who gave us fifteen metres of clothing line. For nothing. And I found a cabinet, which became the bathroom cabinet – the blue cabinet, we used to call it, discovered in the street near Bellenden Rd. We had to scrub off some writing

– graffiti. I wanted to keep it. But it said 'Nobber' and we agreed it would be inappropriate for the kids.

The point is, we put all the cleaning products in the utility room. I'm exhausted explaining this to you. None of this is going how I wanted it to be. I am not going to waste this time explaining about the extension for fucks sake. I cleaned up so you could see – I have kept our end up. I have done my best. Look – look how clean this area of the table is. This table is based on a famous design from the 1960s. Maybe it's bad that I do not know the name or significance of the table.

I cleaned it is the point! I cleaned it with that!

The Host indicates a rag.

I'm sorry for shouting. It's embarrassing, of course. But you wouldn't judge me, would you? I know that. Of course you wouldn't. But, please, don't be shy – I mean, there's no need to hover is there! Ha ha! Sorry. Poor choice of words – hover! What I mean is, you might as well come in. Look, I can arrange some seating for – ah – some of you?

The Host frantically begins to rescue chairs from their upturned and mangled state. He lines them up in a collapsed row, each one falling over as soon as he steadies it. He tries rearranging the order, propping the little chairs against each other, but each time, one of them falls down. He goes through a fixed sequence of propping, and moving, and arranging and rearranging until, eventually each chair is back where it started, toppled and scattered in the craters and the broken floorboards. For example, the chair beside the crater is moved to the space where we are. The chair beside the child's toy kitchen is moved to the crater. The chair in the shadows is moved to the space beside the child's toy kitchen and the chair by the peeling blackout paper is moved to the shadows. It goes on like this until the Host is exhausted, and must sit down to tend to a nosebleed, which we do not think was planned. His blood is shocking to us. Such a thin substance, like black turps. Like smoking oil. We do not move, we can only watch.

I'm not sure this is working. Is this working? I have a lot of this, built up. Things to say – you know? This. Ah-ah. Preamble. Anyway. I'm just trying. I'm determined not to go on about the house for heaven's sake!

Gradually the bleeding stops. The vivid little stream slicks away into the folds of the easy-iron shirts.

I've had almost too long, you know? To prepare what to say to you, at the end. It's like when I played badminton. Is there badminton in the – what do you call it? I want to say, 'out there'. Is there badminton out there?

We do not respond to the question about badminton. The truth is we haven't asked. There might be. There might be anything. All we know for sure is that before you go anywhere else, you must first be in the audience, and hover in the dark, and witness the living flash their bodies and bleed their life at you. You have to listen to them experiencing embarrassment, and not flicker or change or do anything but drift. We can no longer imagine embarrassment. Or shame, or pride or badminton.

No, stupid. How could there be? How would you hold the racket? Anyway, when I played with Martin, or Alessia, or Tahira, or any of them – but mostly those ones who liked to dob the shuttle-cock – you know the type of thing? They would loft the shuttle right up into the air, not to the back of the court even, just high. As high as they could and I would have too much time. I knew exactly what I wanted to do, I could even see the arc of my racket, or the whip of it, but I could never follow through. I would always fluff it. Too much time, you see? Look, this is how I would do it.

The Host performs several dismal badminton shots, shifting his weight through his body. He does not know he is using so much balance. Our mouths would be open if they could be at the audacity of him, his constant revelation of his skin and his bones and his balance. He reignites the nosebleed and is forced to stop.

Sorry. I am very nervous. I had so much I wanted to say, but of course, what would it matter? Over there is the drug I plan to use. I should have used it long ago, but I did not. It felt so stupid. We used to take so many lovely drugs in this kitchen. Well, just weed. Lovely weed. But our friends liked other things, and the friend of ours who sold to us, he died in the street! Not this street, another street. We could not go to his funeral. We had a feast instead, in his honour. I made – I mean, I'm no chef, but I did try some recipes from *PERSIANA*. It was so stupid, half the stuff you couldn't get anymore. I mean, imagine trying to source pomegranate seeds while the world is falling apart. But we did have a feast for him, and we opened some wine. Real wine. I think we opened champagne. Anyway, we had the grains required and other things in the cupboard. There were still supermarkets, but it was all very restricted. It was just us and the kids. We obviously couldn't tell them much, only that a dear friend had gone. A few weeks after that, the siege began, and I hardly cooked at all. Why am I talking about food? It's very painful to talk about food. If you knew what I've been eating. I'm touching the fridge. It's that sort of thing. I touch it, but of course, I cannot open the actual door. Psychologically I mean, I can't. As you know because I told you, I can't go into that corridor, or into the utility room. So, I allow myself just the occasional touch of the fridge – my thin little fingers. *Tapa-tapa*, like that. Not too loud.

The Host is losing focus, and our attention is waning. We have dispersed somewhat, around the room.

What's that you've found? Oh -- ha ha! That's my little nest. That's where I go most days when I think I can hear the guns outside. Although, I have been thinking that perhaps they have all gone. Or have died. There are so many flies, you see? If it's ok, I'll settle in so you can have a look.

The Host climbs in between the broken floorboards near the crater. It looks an impossibly narrow gap. He crawls in elaborately, rolling his shoulders and lifting his eyes up to us. They are deep in their sockets, but bright still, with life.

It's an effort to get in. I must look so ridiculous, but shelter is the most important thing. I suppose this little nest – and the sound construction work we put in on this extension – is the reason I am still here. Still clinging on.

The Host huffs and puffs, breathing in dust.

There. This is where I'm going to sit, you see? When the time comes. I've been building a sort of shelf for my arm to rest on. I've used a few of the classics to build it up. Nothing overly complex. As you can see, I have drawn the line at Nigel Slater. Yes, silly isn't it? Cookery. I often cry if I make the mistake of opening the books. Or I used to. Mostly, and I know this is ridiculous, but I just chat to them. Oh look – it's James Oliver with a tapenade recipe. Here he comes across the road. James Oliver, and he smells of Italy. I would say to him, 'Ahoy James! What have you got there?' And he would say something like, 'Alright? I've got a lovely recipe for mashed up olives. Beautiful it is on a hot day. Mates over. Cold beer. Bit of grissini, bit of black olive tapenade. Black gold I call it! Nicer than caviar, mate, on a hot day with a cold beer. Mates over. Everyone smiling and smoking weed. Better than champagne and caviar that is!'

That's how I imagine James Oliver would talk to me. I call him James because that is my father's name, and I like to say it sometimes. Nobody would ever call my Dad Jamie. But sometimes I imagine how he would respond to it.

You see? It goes like that, in circles. It's black olive tapenade one minute, and then the next, Dad is here and I am asking him how he would have felt if people called him Jamie. Of course, he would have smiled and said it was fine. If a woman loved him, she could call him absolutely anything they liked. His children could call him absolutely anything they liked.

But if I look at the actual recipe for black olive tapenade, I do think I would break down. It has happened before. I dropped a Nigella Lawson one day, and all the pages slipped open. I almost took my death drugs there and then. I had to restrain myself. What if someone comes? I kept thinking. What if she comes back, and she's with the kids? What if they survived? And the end of civilisation was not the actual end. Civilisation or not, I have to be here if they come back. But – it's not them who came. It's you.

The Host turns away abruptly – he seems to be gathering his thoughts. He is still in what he called his nest. We can only see the top of his spine, the spikes of his vertebrae like a dinosaur's scales. Without looking, he starts talking again.

I apologies. I do not normally speak of these things. I swore I would say something memorable.

This is supposed to be a great moment, and I am indulging in tears. It is an indulgence to talk about all of these things. Love and so on. Family. It's insane here in the ruins to think that any of it even existed. These days, it's a source of great pleasure for me. Crying for the sake of crying. And yet, precisely because it gives me pleasure, I don't do it. Such extravagance! Do you still cry? Is there weeping, out there?

The Host is defiant for the duration of a lengthy silence. Some of us disperse further into the kitchen. Entertaining ourselves while the Host lies prone in his hole.

Well, even if there is no weeping out there, I keep it at bay in here. I keep myself as jolly as I can.

Ah, no, stop! Sorry, stop, if you don't mind. So, I should have said it when you first came in. Please don't go into that corner, there. You can go anywhere you like, it's a big kitchen, but I would prefer it if you didn't go there. I use that whole space for very personal, very private, ah, things. Even though technically you can't go anywhere and don't, strictly speaking... well, we might as well address the fact that you may not be real.

We gather again, as a present audience. Attentive, alert. Real.

Sorry, so just don't fucking explore too much, please. Don't keep poking your nose in, if you have noses. I can see that some of you do. Anyway – stop please, because it is just, in fact, too painful.

Surely, I am allowed some privacy. You don't have to see everything. I need a sit down.

The Host climbs out of his little nest. Quickly now, with no showmanship. He retrieves the chair from the shadowed area and brings it into the light. After trying it in several different places, he lays it gently down on its back.

I'll stand, don't worry. You cannot imagine, actually. You cannot imagine what we went through with these chairs. They were supposed to come from Holland. The Netherlands, yeah? And, well, for some reason they were in a warehouse in Utrecht for six months! And then – if you can believe this, they were sent to Canada. London, Canada! Eventually they came back here. They were hand woven from recycled materials. This one's really comfortable. I mean, it's broken now. But before. Oh, we were so glad to finally get them. We had forgotten, and then one day, at the door two huge boxes. I made a simple quiche using the Delia method, of course, for the pastry, and then we sat in the garden. We opened up the bi-folding doors, cranked up the Bose and sat out there in the fading sunlight. It was alright.

The Host pulls a foolish, quite ghoulish face.

It was the sort of indulgence we laughed about, you know, in the early days of all the shit. If they come now, and find us eating quiche in the garden, and drinking this Chablis? Oh, they'd take it away.

Their exuberance, do you remember? Oh, and all the shouting, like everyone was suddenly deaf or something! We used to laugh about that, until they started hammering the doors. Declaring this and that. Using those words that made no sense at all. When they came round to take our food, I couldn't get to the door. They couldn't get in. You see, a lot of the house had collapsed by then. Everything was crumbling except the extension. So they didn't bother coming in. That's how I survived this long. It was rats who took the food in the end. What was left of it, while I was asleep. Mostly, also, the food itself was infested with moths. So the rats ate the moths, and I ate the rats with 'rat-tapenade'! I'll let you figure out the recipe – the key ingredient – for rat tapenade. I don't want to get into it. I want to give up, I really want to end it now.

The Host sits down on the floor. He looks close to expiring. It is unclear if he has finished, but it proves to be a false sunset. He snaps awake and sees us drifting around the room, looking at the kitchen extension.

Oh, you're looking at that crack in the wall. Yeah, good grief! This bit of plaster, I tell you. Ever since we had the work done, it's been like that. They were good builders. We could never work out why that crack kept coming back. I even tried to fill it again after the house fell down around me. Can you imagine? I last gave it some Polyfilla just a few weeks ago, but look! Even now, even though there is no hot water to go to the radiator there below, which I thought was the problem, that crack still comes back.

If humans survive. If humans survive and they come back here, if they excavate me, that's what they will find. That crack. Even if the wall itself has crumbled to ash, the crack will still be there. The crack and our bones, perhaps. A fossil of me, without the fossil of my family, and the things we used to enjoy.

If they ever investigate: We lived here, we loved each other. We voted Labour. We drank champagne whenever we could. What else do you want?

SHEBA

In the corner, in the very corner of the living room, was the hole.

'It's the hole,' said Sheba, on her way to eat from the bowl in the kitchen. 'Hello hole.'

'Hello Sheba,' said the hole.

Now that it had devoured the humans, the hole was friendly most days. Most days, now, the hole was in fact quite polite and didn't really do much.

It was true that the edges of the hole got sticky in the mornings, but only around the horizon of the rim. It wasn't much. It was just this creeping clear gel that seemed to agitate up through the grain of the wood – the oak, was it? – of the floorboards.

You wouldn't call it ideal, living with the hole, but it was easy enough to avoid. Sheba found it easy enough to ignore, now that she was used to it. She'd got used to ignoring things.

'One thing I will say, though, hole. You really upset the balance of the flooring in that corner. It was inconsiderate of you, also, to swallow up the humans in the way that you did. I think you *could* have left them alone.'

'What was that? What did you just say?' asked the hole. It did not speak, but made itself understood in a kind of bitter, angry little way.

'Nothing, nothing. Sorry. I was talking to myself. About mice.'

'Ha ha. You fucking cats. It's always mice with you fucking cats.'

'That's true enough,' said Sheba.

'You going to eat again?' said the hole.

'I suppose.'

'Ha! You cats. You're always fucking eating, aren't you? You fat cunts.'

The hole was a fine one to talk!

Sheba remembered the faces of the humans as they had entered the hole. In particular, she remembered the gaunt, stricken look that the last one had before it went in of its own accord. The hole had paused for a long time – maybe like a whole afternoon, or even a whole day – before it had devoured that last one. Sheba had thought – since it was the youngest, since it was, in fact, a baby – that the hole was going to skip it. She had thought that the baby was going to survive the entire 'hole' situation. She had even started to worry about how she was going to look after it. Momentarily, she'd worried about her ability to produce milk for it and things like that, but it had become clear pretty quickly that she didn't have the necessary resources. It was inevitable, really, that – one way or another – the little human was just going to either get through it or not.

For a couple of hours, there had been a kind of peacefulness about that realisation. While the baby crawled around and wailed, probably looking for its parents or its brother and sister, Sheba had peacefully resigned herself to the reality of the situation. It had wailed for maybe three or four hours, then it seemed to stop for a while and sit there. Then it looked towards the corner, towards the hole, and wailed again.

Of course, Sheba had tried to be of use. She'd tried to make comforting sounds, for instance. She'd tried the occasional nuzzle. But there had been no real line of communication. For a long time, there had just been this stress in the room, that they both felt. It couldn't last.

The baby had been so scared, which was understandable in the circumstances, even for a baby. Before it had devoured the other humans, the hole had stretched them out, like it was making pasta or something, so their arms were useless. Sheba remembered the mother. It was actually really very interesting to watch her trying to grip the floor, the varnished oak floor, with her face. With her nose, ramming it, trying to get a purchase as her teeth buckled. Gurgling because her arms were useless spaghetti. The baby had gurgled too, when it had gone in, eventually. There was nothing Sheba could have done. The humans would not have expected anything of her. She was only a blameless cat. Absolutely none of this was her fault.

'How's the food?' the hole called to her. It sounded sarcastic, but Sheba just lifted her head from the bowl and smiled.

'Fine, thanks!' she sang back. She knew she had to be on her guard, despite the whole politeness thing the hole was trying.

Anyway, that business with the humans, that was all in

the past now. It had been – what? – two or three weeks at least, and the hole was calm. There was still lots of food, magically appearing in her new bowl. A strange-tasting meat she could not put a name on, but it was familiar. Like, homely.

She hadn't forgotten the humans – although already she'd be hard pressed to remember what they looked like in a detailed sense – but without them she had a lot more freedom. It was easier to hang out with Alonso, for instance, which was not something they had been in favour of.

In fact, Alonso would be there soon. Sheba stopped eating. She licked her main paw and began cleaning her body: short licks first – ears and that – then long licks. The long licks were her favourite, what Alonso called the full-service wash. It was exactly like that: she was enjoying the luxury of being washed, and also the luxury of having someone she cared about to look after.

As she washed, she thought more about Alonso and the words he used. She liked him because, like her, he had a lasting attachment to human concepts. He spoke in this human way – a lot of, 'First Class'. A lot of, 'There's Nothing to Fear But Fear Itself'.

'Seize The Day'. That's what he said when he was leaving you unexpectedly, or if you saw him on the wall, but he didn't have time to stop: 'Going for a little walk,' he'd say. 'You Seize The Day.'

She finished paddling behind her ears and got into the main action of the wash.

When Alonso arrived, he didn't bother to come in. She just heard him mewling outside. Saying good afternoon to a thick swarm of flies.

'Come and look, Al!' She had called out to him.

'Sorry, kitten. No can do.'

'But I want you to see the hole in the floor,' she said to his blur on the other side of the cat flap.

'No point. There's one at mine, just the same.'

'So then why have you come over?'

'Oh, I have something to show you!' he said.

That was Alonso. Always something to show you. Last time that meant he wanted to try sex, and that had gone alright, but in a park? It was not her preferred thing.

'Can't you show it to me in here?' she said.

'No.'

'I didn't really like the setting last time.'

'It's not that! I'm not here for that. Come on, I'm getting a nose ache out here. What's that awful smell?'

She pushed through the cat flap to join Alonso in the stairwell. About the smell, she said, 'Bleach, scented with pine.'

'It's awful,' said Alonso.

She had to agree with him there. It really was a horrendous smell. Sam – the human male in her home – would always buy this bleach scented with pine. He drove them all mad with it. The baby would be crying. 'Why is the baby crying?' Sam would say. 'Because of the pine-scented bleach,' Sheba would say, but of course Sam just took it personally that she was attempting to communicate at all. He would say, 'Fucking cat now!' and shove her out of the cat flap. Sometimes grabbing her and taking her all the way down to the main entrance and shoving her through *that* cat flap.

When the holes started opening up in the flats, Sam tried to poison all the floor areas with pine bleach. As if it would somehow kill the holes. He poured it all down the stairs. Sam the male human did a lot of things that made no sense in those last days.

'Come on,' Alonso said. 'We need to get going.'

'So you've said, but where?'

'It's The Journey That Matters,' Alonso replied. 'More Than The Destination.'

As they walked down the echoing stairs, through the blare of bleachy smells, Sheba stopped to urinate by the door.

'That your normal pissing place?' Alonso asked, quite friendly.

'Yes – I can't stand that smell.'

'Humans!' he said. 'What went on in their heads? No wonder they all went in! Idiots. Not equipped to survive even a basic hole.'

'I miss them sometimes,' Sheba said.

'That's because you're too kind, Sheba. Hardly even like a cat at all.'

'Meow,' she said, in her best human voice.

'Meowfzzzzzz!' Alonso said, impersonating humans as they impersonated a cat hissing.

Alonso was so funny. She was relieved when they went out through the broken entrance of the flats, into sweet St William's Square.

'Where are the others?' she said.

'You'll see,' Alonso said, turning around and then away again with a flick of his tail.

'Alonso, I don't feel like going far today, OK?'

'No. Not OK,' said Alonso, moving away, striking out across the deserted grasses of the square.

The town was soaked underfoot and there was this awful fresh blinding sun. She followed Alonso with her eyes raging from the light, glad she could just track the angles he cut through the town. She had realised by now where they were going, and thought at least the journey wouldn't take long. Alonso took them on and off walls, under bruised-looking fences, barely deviating from a straight line.

In the beginning, when the humans first vanished from her flat, she had started meandering further and further from home. Other cats were doing the same, she saw them sometimes gathering, which she found frankly strange. Too many other cats became a real bore after a while.

But Alonso loved to roam, and for some reason he started coming to collect her or planning to meet her on a daily basis. It was great sometimes but other times it was also exhausting, especially when he would turn a nice walk into a massive social event.

The gatherings had recently taken on more structure and they were getting really anti-social and dull.

She liked being close to home. And, if she was honest, she was kind of comfortable with the hole now, and enjoyed their stupid conversations. She was pretty sure that somehow the hole in her place was the one providing food for her. Those sweet soft chunks of meat in jelly and gravy. She was salivating when Alonso muttered, 'Keep Up Slow Coach.'

'I'm really not up for a long walk today, Alonso.'

She could smell another hole as they went past a row of houses, they each had their own variation, but always the general overtone of vomit and digestive fluids. She figured that the smell came from that moisture around their rims. Every hole must have that wetness now, she thought. Like, the lips of a sick animal.

'It's A New Dawn,' Alonso said. 'It's A New Day. And I'm Feeling Good,' Then he mimed, with his tongue, the action of eating a luxury yoghurt.

He had done this same routine the first time they met, and it had been pretty funny that one time, but now he seemed to do it constantly. He would do it, and then he would look at her, making her feel obliged to nod along. Sometimes he wouldn't do the 'And I'm Feeling Good,' bit from the advert, but instead leave a silence and stare at her, so she would have to do it.

'You love those songs,' Alonso said to her.

'Hmm. Yeah, I guess,' she said, although she really only paid passing attention to the songs from the television.

'You miss the humans! It's so tragic and sweet,' Alsonso said. 'Actually, wait here.'

Alonso made her wait while he pissed against a wall. Sheba was struck by his sharp, fierce smell. Like a wood spike, snagging her throat as he sprayed against some mortar. She made a mental note to try and edge Alonso out of her life. She felt like there was a chance for her to be free. She had a nice flat, and once the bleach smell went away, she could invite someone else over. She didn't know who, but someone she had more in common with. In the meantime, it was Alonso and his annoyingly long, annoyingly paced walks.

They were now at Malthouse, a long lane that dissected what Sheba thought of as 'her' side – where there were flats and tall buildings and a lot of noise and fights. The good stuff, she had always thought of it – the real life. On the other side of Malthouse were the big houses, the lazy cul-de-sacs, the stabbing smell of bleach and synthetic perfumes.

She had crossed Malthouse many times before the holes came, but never considered going along the lane, up that hill like they were doing now.

This journey made her nervous every time, but she went anyway. On both sides the humans had planted trees, sycamores and cherries, full of leaves and blossoms. Sheba let the soft white smells please her. The gaudy, flabby fruit of the petals. The clacking green leaves of the sycamore trees. She was still suffering with the sun in her eyes though. It was blaring off the wet road, and Alonso's pace was irritating now, his insistence that they were going somewhere, as opposed to strolling together. It was as if she was making them late, but Sheba was not late. She had made no appointment.

'Keep up will you!'

'Just slow down. What's the point in rushing now? I've agreed to come to the park. I've agreed to come with you, there's no need to rush is there?'

'You're so slow.'

'Whatever.'

She was more than capable of this speed but, because he had started ahead, she was always catching up. His voice in the distance, repeating his complaints about her speed with ever increasing regularity.

She lowered her eyes to the pavement, saw her smoky black legs jabbing into the light and out again until they reached the dew slabbed grass of Archery Fields.

There were others already there. More than she had ever seen in one place.

'You didn't say it was a gathering,' she hissed to Alonso, but he didn't reply. He was already moving towards the main cluster of other cats. He was doing this thing where he would greet a cat, and then both he and the other cat would do a very specifically feline motion. Not something you saw often, a kind of wild action.

Sheba listened and looked around for cats she could trust. She picked out the soft bass voices of Toni and Adonnis, the heavy cats from near her own place. Gladis was with them. Gladis was a house cat until the holes came, but now she was everywhere you looked.

'Alright guys,' she said approaching the three of them. They stopped talking and turned away from her.

She scanned the field for Alonso. He was in a group of four or five cats, which was just weird for him, and he seemed to be entertaining them. She could hear them responding in a way that was unlike how Alonso normally talked. They were reacting in almost completely cat dialects. There were no human leftovers in their talk at all.

Sheba had been noticing this, an abandonment of human concepts and words. A movement towards an almost entirely feline discourse. Of course, in feline discourse there is no concept of the feline or the non-feline. Or of discourse. There is just this cat-ness. So what Alonso had actually been saying to them, was only intelligible if you ignored the domestic element of your domestic cat-ness altogether. He was describing a scenario that was to do with stillness. The joke, or the comedy of it, was that in order to describe the stillness, Alonso had to move, but he moved to another kind of stillness. At one point the wind changed, and Alonso released an improvised kind of emission – not spraying, but somehow making the smell. The smell also spoke of the fractional line between movement and non-movement and stillness and still-movement.

It was quite a dry joke, but the cats were loving it. Sheba didn't really recognise them all. There was one from the cul-de-sacs on the other side of Malthouse from Sheba.

Her name was Primrose, but Sheba suspected that calling her by that name now would be a mistake.

'Alonso,' she said. 'What's going on?'

Alonso didn't say anything. He acted as though the word Alonso was not even a sound he recognised.

'Fuckssake, man,' she said. 'I am going home.'

But she didn't move. There was a change in the air. Suddenly, all eyes were on her. What had previously been a sort of loose gathering, was now a fairly organised group, and they were slowly forming a circle around her.

'I heard it was bad,' The cat formerly known as Primrose said. 'But I didn't realise she was actually calling you a man.' Several other cats hissed and laughed at this, all in feline dialect. No human accents at all.

Ignoring this comment, Sheba spoke directly to Alonso again.

'Come on, Alonso, why have you brought me here? This place is weird. It's weird all these cats together.'

Alonso did not answer, but he prowled over to her, joining her in the centre of the wide circle.

'Let's walk,' he said. He led her along the grass towards the blank end of Archery fields, where the large outdoor hole was.

'What's the deal, Al,' she said. As they walked, the rest of the cats moved with them, keeping a movable clearing around Sheba and Alonso. 'We normally fight these fucking idiots, or just leave them to their stupid nonsense. Why are you huddling around with them? What's that fucking voice you put on with them?'

'We have been conversing with the Hole,' Alonso said. As though it was the obvious answer. 'Every cat here has been conversing with the external Hole – the outside Hole – here at Archery Fields.'

'Alonso, please don't talk like that, like you're announcing something. It makes me feel on edge.'

'We have been conversing with the Hole. The Hole tells us things. The humans are all gone. That was the first stage. Everything human must also follow. These are the words of the Hole. Everything humanity stood for must also be dismissed. Cats are human, the Hole has said. Cats are too human.'

'Cats are human? That's ridiculous.'

'We told the Hole that cats are not human. We agreed that it's possible some human traits have been passed to us, through no fault of our own, because of our upbringing. But we are grateful to the holes. The holes feed us and will continue to help us be better cats, if we make a small sacrifice in return. So – we must cast our most human cat into the Hole.'

'Right, well, that's not me is it? I'm more cat than most of you. What about Shelag? She's got an actual hat on.'

The cat called Shelag hissed loudly. The other cats all hissed loudly. A cat called Boniface urinated unintentionally on the ground.

'I'm not going in that Hole,' Sheba said.

Yet, she was following Alonso towards it. She couldn't see it, but she could hear it rumbling, talking to her the way the one at home had talked to the humans.

'Come on then lovely-lovely-lovely, come on then. You're so sweet. You're such a lovely thing. You can have anything you like, come on then, come on then.'

'Guys, please!' she said. 'Can't you see, I'm not a human? This is insane!'

But everyone that Sheba looked at turned their faces away. She didn't want to keep walking, but she could not stop. She thought of the hole back home, the baby crawling in quite calmly, wanting to find its parents.

'I want this to stop now please. I'd like to go home now.' Sheba said.

Nobody spoke – nobody even moved. Sheba was locked into Alonso's step – she didn't have the power to break away. She followed him through the shadows under the conker trees. She followed him across the rugby pitch, over the half-way line and then the dead ball line. Scrags of torn leaves skipped by, making harsh sounds of the breeze.

'Alonso, I'm asking you. I'm begging you, man, please make it stop?'

'She called him a man again!' someone hissed. 'In the Hole, in the Hole!'

Alonso just sighed like she was a fool. And she was! She was just following him, and all the others were turning away. They were muttering, and she felt alone.

At the far end of Archery Fields, the ground ended in darkness. An enormous Hole. It was just like the one at home only bigger. The only one that had appeared in the open, this was thought of as the last active hole.

She circled round, but it was too late. She was surrounded now by all of the other cats. Alonso drifted off to the left and sat, licking himself. Cleaning himself as the cats crowded in. Sheba could hear the enormous Hole talking to her, making deep, low moans.

'It's easier if you just go in,' said Alonso softly.

'But.'

'Just get in the fucking Hole,' said Gladis, with Toni purring in affirmation. 'Get the fuck in the Hole.'

'But – but, why? Why me?' Sheba asked, her voice now raspy with defeat. 'Why should it be me?'

Nobody answered. They closed in, forcing her movements without touching, as she gingered backwards and felt that grease under her pads, the lip of the massive Hole at the edge of the park. Inside it, somewhere, she could hear the snuffling sound of the memory of a human. The wet clomp of her jaw, trying her hardest to cling onto the world while the rest of her stretched away into the dark.

ACKNOWLEDGEMENTS

This is my first book, it has taken ages, and I have had a lot of help, so there are a lot of people to thank.

I am firstly grateful for the constant emotional support of what started as a compact unit, and then became a beautiful big sprawling family – especially Liz Leck (my wonderful mum), Laurie (when you were here and also now that you aren't), Rod, Judith, Uncle Kit, my brothers, my sisters, my children, my dad, and my French family – especially Georges and Jos Fournet.

I am indebted specifically to the following people for their time, patience, and care of me as a writer:

I wouldn't have been confident to write any of this without the wisdom and generosity of Naomi Wood. Likewise, I'd be completely lost without Jack Underwood and Holly Pester. Without you guys, it would just be me standing about, saying 'I don't know what to do.'

Thank you Tom Pester for always understanding what I mean, and for being an influence of such honesty and positivity that I hardly feel worthy.

Huge thanks to Kevin Riddle, Evie Wyld, Charlie Tittle, Rachel Payant, Kate Wasserberg, Kate Everitt, Laura Voyle, Andy Galletly, Dan Bibby, Charlie Turnbull, Ben Gardiner, Tony Volker, Ed Harkness, Hannah Nixon, Gabriel Gbadamosi, Nick Kiddle, and Bryn Tittle for the years of being the most treasured kind of readers: the ones who take early drafts without flinching, and read them like they are real things, and fill them with hope.

Thank you to Luke Neima, Eleanor Chandler, and Josie Mitchell, who have all treated my work ('Rachel Reaches Out' and 'All Silky and Wonderful') so carefully at *Granta*. Dominic Jaeckle and his wonderful

Hotel magazine for publishing 'If yes, then please explain your answer'. And Craig Taylor for rolling with the weirdness and publishing 'Mother's Day Card from a Wooden Object' in *Five Dials*.

When you get no other money help, good employers and clients are everything. So, cheers to all at Goldsmiths University. Unending glory to Ruth Jamieson, thanks to Jay Johnston, and lastly thanks to David E. Rutter who, as I write this under lockdown, made it still possible to feed my family.

Thank you to Cathryn Summerhayes, my agent whose mere presence in the last couple of years has stopped me giving up more times that I have managed to tell her. Thank you to all at Boiler House – especially Jasmin Kirkbride – a miracle-worker, and Philip Langeskov, my editor, who now knows more about me than he probably bargained for, and has done as he promised with this work, which was to make my stupid dreams come true.

Thank you Émilie, Orson, and Cosima for everything.